SEARCHING FOR FOREVER

SEARCHING FOR FOREVER

by

Emily Smith

2014

SEARCHING FOR FOREVER
© 2014 By Emily Smith. All Rights Reserved.

ISBN 13: 978-1-62639-186-4

This Trade Paperback Original Is Published By
Bold Strokes Books, Inc.
P.O. Box 249
Valley Falls, NY 12185

First Edition: September 2014

Credits
Editor: Shelley Thrasher
Production Design: Stacia Seaman
Cover Design by Sheri (graphicartist2020@hotmail.com)

To Mom—forever my biggest fan.

Chapter One

Natalie, you've got a lower-extremity injury in room 3. She's twenty-five. Slipped on a patch of ice coming into the hospital."

Judy, one of the older nurses on staff, had been at Northwood since my father's heyday. I remember seeing her in the cafeteria when I'd come visit him as a kid. Now, she had to listen to me—order my tests, do my procedures, give my medications. Somehow, that never sat quite right with me.

"Coming into the hospital? What was she doing here?"

"She's our new in-house medic. First day. Welcome to Northwood, right? Should have known you'd be on today."

I rolled my eyes at her, knowing my reputation as the department's harbinger of doom and gloom would probably never escape me. In our tiny, ten-bed facility, I once oversaw two cardiac arrests within two hours. I was what we, in medicine, call "a black cloud," someone who seems to attract disaster no matter what they do. It would make sense, then, that CarolAnne Thompson would break her right ankle on her first day in the ER, during my shift.

She was young and looked even younger. A thick head of short, auburn hair sat disheveled above brilliant green eyes that seemed so, so much older.

"CarolAnne, I'm Dr. Jenner." After so many years, I still felt a little uncomfortable referring to myself that way. Dr. Jenner, Dr. Marcus Jenner, was my father—the overachieving stroke of brilliance that moved gracefully from the cradle to the bedside without so much as needing a calculator. At least that was how the rest of the world saw him.

"Call me Charlie. Please. Nobody but my grandmother calls me CarolAnne." She flashed a clean, white smile, which reminded me she hadn't even lived long enough to damage her teeth yet, and two asymmetrically placed dimples appeared under her strong cheekbones.

"Okay then. Charlie. It looks like you've got—"

"A right tib-fib fracture, I'm guessing?"

If she hadn't smiled again, my intrigue might have felt more like disdain and annoyance. But something in the way she spoke made her seem strong and self-assured.

"Yes. A medial tibia fracture, if you want to get specific." I smiled back, careful not to let on just how impressive I already found her. "We'll get you in a boot, set you up with some crutches and some Percocet, and you'll be good to go."

"Thank you, Dr. Jenner."

"And, while we're on the topic, no EMS for six weeks."

Her face fell a bit, as she tried to feign understanding. But I imagined medicine was everything to Charlie, much as it had been to me. As a child, I'd sit in my father's study while he went over, in unadulterated detail, article after article, leading to complex lessons about the circulatory system and the brain that, at the time, both intrigued and perplexed me. I'd wait all day for this session, knowing it was some of the most significant time I'd be able to spend with him. It didn't take me long to notice that same spark in Charlie when she talked about medicine, and I wondered what brought her here.

"Take care," I said, walking briskly to the door, chart in hand, eyes straight ahead. "Oh, and Charlie," her focused gaze was still locked my way when I turned around again, "welcome to Northwood."

❖

Weeks had passed, and I slowly made my way into the hospital's locker room, large cup of black coffee in hand, and changed into a set of the dark-blue scrubs that made up most of my wardrobe. Nurses and doctors and house cleaners and whoever else knew me politely greeted me with the kind of forced enthusiasm usually reserved for doctors, and for some reason, I was more grateful than ever to be there. My daughter Sammy was six and was struggling with even the simplest daily tasks.

Before Sammy was born, medicine hovered at the enormous forefront of my life, with my husband Peter, our comfortable Northwood four-bedroom home, and our Irish setter, Max, acting as cushioning support—a vehicle to feed what I loved the most. For years, I was a doctor. Then, I became first a doctor and then a wife. And, when Samantha was born, premature, at 4 pounds, 8 ounces, I became a mother, then a doctor, and finally a wife.

Peter—trying to move her along at an impossibly fast speed while never ceasing to spoil her—was tired and cantankerous. I hadn't had a chance to pay the mortgage, or the utility bills, or Sammy's charges we'd accrued from her last hospital stay. And last night I'd managed to fall asleep for only a few fitful hours on the big chair in our den, sipping a tall glass of chardonnay and reading an article on advanced airway management in the obese patient. I woke up at four a.m. with no other prompting than a diet-shake infomercial and Max licking my fingertips.

I was glad to be at work.

"What do you have for me, Tim?" I asked, sitting purposefully in the wheeled desk chair in front of my computer.

"Not too much. A COPDer. Gave him some albuterol and he's doing fine now. Oxygen around 95. Respiratory's in there now. A thirty-year-old with chest pain. Negative troponin, negative EKG. Just looks muscular. Oh, and a hip fracture that's waiting on surgery."

"Fair enough. Thanks."

"Try not to kill anyone today, okay, kid?" Dr. Tim Banks still thought of me as my father's daughter. He was a spry seventy-two, one year from retirement. Most of his patients now saw him as a fossil. Nonetheless, Tim had been at Northwood for decades. He'd earned the right to demean me.

"Tim," I asked, as casually as I could manage, "have you worked with the new medic yet?"

"Who? Charlie?"

"Yeah, Charlie."

"A little. She's good. I've seen a lot of those guys in my day, but this one knows her stuff. She's a good one to have on your team."

I nodded thoughtfully and turned to my work.

After a few more sips of coffee, I was on my way down the short hallway to see the older man with COPD. I spotted her right away, sitting next to a young woman in room 9, holding her arm gently, ready to draw her blood. She wore dark-blue pants with pockets on the sides and a heather-gray-collared shirt. Her hair, auburn and still intentionally disheveled, was bright with subtle highlights from the fluorescents overhead. Charlie pierced the woman's arm with the same humble self-assurance I'd seen in room 3, six weeks to the day earlier. Realizing just how long I'd been standing outside the young woman's room, I quickly flipped through the COPD patient's chart with mock determination.

Only the sound of the shuffling papers made Charlie look up from her task. She grinned so effortlessly I had to glance around to see if she had anyone or anything else to smile at. She didn't. And, just as effortlessly, she returned to her work.

❖

Charlie's presence had shaken me in a way I couldn't quite pinpoint. I spent the next few hours submerging myself in work, and by the time she approached my desk that afternoon, I'd almost managed to go on with life as usual. Almost.

"Dr. Jenner? I'm the new in-house medic…I…"

"Charlie." I jumped, probably far more eagerly than I'd intended.

"Oh, you remember me." She blushed a fiery red, and for just a moment, her experience and confidence in medicine was a guise that lay beneath her young exterior.

"I remember all my patients." A lie. "Especially those who work with me." Less of a lie, but a lie regardless.

"Well, anyway, I have this patient in 10. She has a long history. Emphysema, old MI, some stents placed…A few minutes ago, I was helping her up to the bathroom and she dropped her sats down to the low 70s."

"How'd she look?"

"Terrible. Diaphoretic, dusky. Textbook. I upped her oxygen to 6 on the cannula, but I'm worried."

"I've seen this woman before. Some Solu-Medrol usually works. I'll write the orders."

"Thanks, Dr. Jenner," Charlie said, the same breath of confidence sweeping over her.

"Call me Natalie. Please. Only my grandmother calls me Dr. Jenner." She turned quickly, moving toward the med room, as I spun my chair back toward my computer screen, suppressing a delighted smile.

❖

Northwood is a small hospital. It's small in its number of beds, and even smaller in regard to the gossip that goes around. Over the following weeks, I was told more unsolicited facts about our newest medic than I'd ever thought possible. At twenty-five, Charlie was about thirteen years my junior. She'd been a medic since, essentially, the moment she graduated from high school.

And, after spending years jumping trucks in Spanish Harlem on her weekends off from college, she'd had enough of the streets and wanted to move inside. Rumor had it she'd applied, and been accepted, to Dartmouth's medical school, on nearly a full scholarship. But this was years ago, and I never heard why she ended up with me.

I heard other kinds of gossip too—gossip that took a more personal form, gossip I wasn't fully comfortable with.

The fact that Charlie was gay wasn't a secret. She never tried to hide her sexual identity from anyone, save maybe her eighty-year-old patients who asked her about her "husband." That was all I'd heard, though. And even that, somehow, felt vaguely inappropriate.

Chapter Two

You don't forget patients like Gerald Green—the ones who come in walking, talking, and then, in literally an instant, they're dying.

The weather was a grotesque cocktail of sleet, snow, ice, rain, and nearly anything else a Rhode Island winter can throw at you. Roads were glassy and slick, and the waiting room was filling up with minor car crashes, kids with fevers, and drug-seekers afraid of running out of Vicodin before the storm let up.

Forty-seven-year-old Gerald was actually not looking to be a patient that night. He was there with his older sister, whose name I never learned, because she'd been complaining of chest pain for several days. Growing concerned, he drove her himself, not wanting her out alone in the weather. Gerald had no complaints. But as he stood at the triage desk, filling out paperwork for his sister, he suddenly turned ashen and fell to the ground.

I was sitting at my desk, charting the last several routine patients I'd seen that night, trying to gather my second wind for the inevitable swell of traumas and shoveling victims that would greet me by midnight.

"Dr. Jenner to triage, please, Dr. Jenner." A paging system seemed sort of superfluous in such a small place. Still, it wasn't every day I was paged to the waiting area.

As I passed through the doors at the end of the hallway, the growing crowd at the desk caused me to pick up my tired pace. A group comprised of nurses and a few curious onlookers circled something I couldn't see, hands furiously grabbing for things and pushing each other out of the way.

"We've got a code here," one of the nurses said, stepping away from the chaos.

The familiar quickening of my heart rate and slight rush of heat to my face kicked off a cascade of emotions that ended with a feeling of innate urgency. "What happened?"

A small pathway of bodies parted for me as I made my way to Gerald. He was young, only five years older than I was, and as close to death as a person can get.

"He was just standing at the desk when I saw him go down. CPR's been going on for about five minutes now. He's been in V-fib on the monitor. Shocked him once right off the bat without any change." Charlie's face gleamed with sweat as she straddled the man and compressed his chest. Judy was kneeling at his head, forcing air into his deflated lungs.

"Okay. Somebody get access? He needs a line and some epi."

"He's got two 18 gauge IVs in already. One round of epi's in, but I thought you might want to see him before we move him back to the trauma room."

Charlie was good. Her reputation hadn't been a hoax. The speed and agility with which she was working on Gerald caused me to wonder, again, what had happened to Dartmouth. But the thought soon dissolved as I concentrated on the task at hand.

"Let's get him on a backboard, and get him out of here. This isn't a free show."

We worked on Gerald Green for nearly an hour before calling his big sister back to Trauma 10 to tell her he was dead. To tell her that, although he'd never had so much as a cold in his life, it was apparently his time to go. Bullshit. Medical-school ethics-class, grief-counseling bullshit. When the monitors were shut off and the ventilator was disconnected, I took my cup of coffee and climbed the stairs to the roof. I'd discovered Northwood's helipad at ten years old, when I'd come to work with my father and he'd dump me off with one of the candy stripers. Somehow, sitting on a tipped trash can, hoping a med-flight would land, became my favorite refuge. At thirty-eight, I still used it.

I couldn't let Gerald go, even as I nudged open the door to the roof, coffee in one hand, the other buried deep in my jacket pocket. The wind ripped at my exposed cheeks, and fat, heavy snow toppled to the ground. I didn't care. There was too much for me down in the ER right then. I just couldn't go back to suturing a drunken idiot's lacerated forehead when I couldn't save the Gerald Greens of the world. It would dissipate, of course. The anger and fear…it would all ebb as I stood on the helipad and watched the snowflakes spiral out of a black sky. It always did.

It was a while before I realized I wasn't alone. A shadow, just a few inches taller than my own, stood smoking a cigarette on the corner of the giant "H." I was hesitant to approach, not because I was afraid but because I wanted to be alone. Still, something led me to anyway. I followed the path of the cigarette smoke, the orange tip acting as a beacon to whomever I'd find on the other side of it.

"Charlie?" She stood, eyes locked to the ground, cigarette ash burning almost to her gloved fingers. "Charlie." Then she emerged from whatever reality she'd been visiting. Maybe it was a reality where we'd saved Gerald Green. Where forty-two-year-olds didn't just drop dead in your waiting room. Where a couple of little kids didn't become fatherless because an aorta decided to dissect itself after only a few decades. Maybe it was my reality too.

"Oh. Hi."

"What are you doing up here? It's freezing."

"I could probably ask you the same thing. But I won't, because I have a feeling I know the answer."

We stood silently for a long few moments, the harsh cold a bittersweet reminder that we were, in fact, still here. Gerald Green wasn't. But we were.

"You know, smoking will kill you," I said, my lips shivering.

"So will dissecting aortas." Her gaze remained focused and determined, in a way that reminded me of some of the disciplined surgeons I'd seen in the operating room.

"Point taken."

The silence filled in around us once again, leaving me feeling appropriately empty and reflective. I was comfortable though and, somehow, happy I wasn't alone.

"You know," Charlie said, grinding the butt of her Camel with her steel-toed boot, "I only smoke when I lose someone."

"I was only teasing you. Really. I'm not here to be your mother." Although "mother" felt like the least of any possible association to her.

"Does it ever get any easier?" she asked, hesitantly. "You know, the Geralds?"

I paused a moment, feeling as if my answer needed to be able to fix whatever was broken inside of her that night.

"No. No it never does." Through the shadows cast by the streetlights below us, I saw her usually brilliant green eyes sink to the ground and the corners of her mouth fall innocently. "But it's not supposed to get easier. When it gets easy to lose someone… that's when you know it's time to move on. You've been in this business too damn long when Gerald Green doesn't make you want to scream, or cry, or hit someone."

"I can't picture you hitting anyone," she said, with a small but relieving smile that seemed to lift me up in ways I hadn't been in weeks—not at home with Peter, not in the trauma rooms, not anywhere.

"Are you kidding? I can kick some ass if I need to. You should see me when some of these drug-seekers get out of hand."

She laughed loudly from somewhere inside her I hadn't seen all night—and I thought it sounded something like healing.

"Okay, so maybe not here in Northwood. But back in Phoenix, during my residency, I took down a few." She laughed some more. "No, really! I swear!" I turned quickly and began feigning punches. "Of course," I stopped, with a soft smile, "I'm not as young as I used to be."

"Oh, come on. You're not that old," Charlie mumbled, and I was sure I saw a flash of something in her smile that reminded me of coyness. "Champ." She swung a right hook into the air in front of me, looking at me hard for what felt like hours. Unconsciously, I found myself looking back. Just as hard. Maybe harder.

"I better get back downstairs." She finally spoke, breaking the grasp she was holding with her eyes. "They're going to start looking for me."

"Yeah. Me too." And we took off, slowly, through the heavy roof door, down the four flights of stairs, neither of us saying another word.

❖

What did Charlie Thompson know about me? Did she know about my predictable, handsome husband? Or my sweet daughter? Or our cute split-level on Beech Street with a swimming pool? Had she heard about my father—how could she not have? His supposed legacy was like a virus around Northwood. You couldn't avoid it.

And if she knew the exterior—knew what the nurses or the other medics, or Tim, or anyone else knew—did she know the truth? Just how much of my life was evident beneath the role I wanted to play: Natalie Jenner, MD, loving mother, brilliant physician, devoted…adoring…happy wife…

But there was nothing extraordinary about Peter. He was mediocre in just about every plane of his life—except in his ability to love our daughter. And by the time I finally realized this, Sammy had become what held us together in a large and necessary way.

Charlie didn't wear a ring on her finger; she didn't have any outward symbol that she was committed to anyone or anything, other than medicine. Still, as I sat in my rolling desk chair in front of a scan of a right humerus late one Monday morning, I wondered, who was she? What was she hiding from when she immersed herself in trauma, destruction, and all of the most horrific parts of humanity? Or maybe that was just me. Maybe Charlie was able to use medicine as a career. Maybe it was something to leave here in the hospital when she went home to someone, a woman, who made her happy. Maybe, for Charlie, other people's disasters simply paid the bills although, somehow, I doubted it.

❖

"Nat, come down here. Sammy's sick again." Peter's voice came through in muffled waves up to my office on the top floor, where I sat at my computer researching special-needs daycares for our daughter. Peter needed to go back to work, not so much because we needed the money, but because I was afraid I'd kill him if I had to stay home with him any longer.

Sammy brought me something I loved even more than being a physician. But she had grown slowly, requiring constant love and attention, and by the time she was two, she finally reached the size of an infant. For the first few years, she didn't speak and hardly cried. She needed more than any daycare or nanny could offer. So Peter reluctantly sold his tiny electrician business. Day after day, I went into the ER, working long, arduous shifts, which seemed to hold me together in some large and necessary way while Peter stayed home with Sammy, playing the part of stay-at-home-dad and family martyr.

For years, the hospital had been enough of a twisted paradise for me to escape to when my home threatened to swallow me alive, but recently, it just hadn't seemed like enough. I loved Sammy, and I loved Peter, for all of our shortcomings. But on some days—most days—it was all too much.

"Can't you deal with it? I'm in the middle of something."

"I think it's bad. She's bleeding again."

I hurried downstairs to find Sammy lying on the couch in Peter's arms, somnolent and waxy eyed.

"What happened?"

"She was in the bathroom…there was more blood…I think we should…"

"Get her dressed. Pack a bag. I'm calling the hospital." I moved to the cordless phone and immediately dialed the number to Northwood's Emergency Department.

"Maybe we should just call John McGee," Peter suggested hesitantly. John was only a pediatrician, and she needed the emergency room. I brashly showed him the palm of my hand and pointed to the phone's receiver.

"It's Natalie Jenner. Hi. Yes, I'm bringing my daughter in… Another GI bleed…About ten minutes or so. Please let Tim or Jack know. Thank you." I hung up and grabbed a bag of Sammy's things from the bedroom.

"I'll get her some Cheerios. She hasn't had dinner yet," Peter said, scooping Sammy up in one arm and heading toward the kitchen.

"Peter, she has a GI bleed. She can't eat."

"I'm sorry we didn't all go to medical school, okay?"

"It's fine! Just grab her coat. I'll bring the car around."

An overwhelming relief washed over me as the neon EMERGENCY sign lit up the sky on the horizon—not only because of my sick daughter, but because of the sanctuary the hospital offered. It was always like coming up for air.

"Park the car. I'll take her in," I said, jumping out of the driver's seat in front of the main entrance and helping Sammy out of the back. "Come on, sweetie. We're going to see Uncle Tim again, okay? We've got to get you feeling better."

Once we were inside, two of the younger nurses greeted me at the desk. "Room 6, Natalie.

One of them picked up the phone and called back to the main department, tension in her voice. "We're going to need labs and an IV right away…someone grab Charlie."

I'd already found myself looking around the department for her. Somehow, I felt better just knowing she was nearby.

"When Peter gets here, will you tell him where we are?" One of the nurses nodded softly, as I turned and carried Sammy into the room.

❖

A tentative knock caught my attention as I flipped through the television channels in the tiny exam room, trying to find cartoons. Peter sat in a chair next to the bed, holding one of Sammy's sweaty hands. No matter how many times we went through this, he always had the same petrified expression in his eyes. I understood. In spite of all my years of training, it never got any easier to see her suffer.

"Natalie?"

"Oh, hi, Charlie. Come on in. Please." The same sense of overwhelming relief I'd felt driving in once again caught me and rose into my chest. I hardly knew her, and yet everything in me told me I could trust her.

She was carrying a tray filled with needles and tubes, standing taller than I knew she really was, with long sleeves pushed up high to reveal strong arms. With a sympathetic smile, Charlie sat on the stool next to the bed and looked into Sammy's frightened face.

"Hi, Sammy," she said, as if just the two of them were there. "My name's Charlie. I'm a friend of your mom."

Sammy narrowed her eyebrows and buried her face into my neck, leaving me with my eyes locked on Charlie.

"I have a question for you, Sammy. It's a very important question that only you can answer. Can you help me?" Intrigued, Sammy peeked out from under my chin and turned toward her. "Do you know who this is?" Charlie reached into the pocket on the side of her pants and pulled out a small stuffed doll. I could only watch with awe as my daughter finally smiled. "This is SpongeBob. He's a good friend of mine. But I had a feeling you already knew that. Could you watch him for me? I'm pretty busy tonight, and he gets awful lonely. Could you take care of him for me while I work? Please?"

Charlie pouted out her lips and held the toy in front of her, waiting for Sammy to react. I sighed and laughed a little to myself as the beautiful little girl in my lap nodded several times and grabbed the doll.

As Charlie gathered her supplies for the procedure, Sammy sat contentedly in my arms, making SpongeBob's legs bend and twist while Peter looked on uneasily.

"Thank you," I mouthed silently, and offered Charlie the most indebted smile I could muster. Her face flushed and she brought her focus back to the work at hand.

"Okay, Sammy. Now I have to give you a shot. I know it's going to hurt a lot, and it's going to be scary…" Sammy looked up from her toy as her eyes welled with tears, and her mouth began to tremble. "But then, it'll all be over. And you'll feel so much better. And Mommy's going to stay with you, and, of course, SpongeBob will be here too. But he's going to be scared. So you need to be extra brave for him too, okay?" Sammy pondered the request for a moment, and then, with eyes drying, she nodded with resolution. "Good."

Charlie caught my eye and signaled to the needle in her hand. I nodded quickly.

"Sammy, did you know that SpongeBob loves balloons? I bet you like balloons too. What's your favorite color balloon?"

Sammy was watching Charlie's soothing, confident smile so intently, she hardly cried as the tiny needle pinched her arm. "That was it, sweetheart. All done!" A short string of tears spilled from Sammy's eyes, but only for a moment. And then she was smiling and laughing. And so was I.

"You were so good. SpongeBob feels much better now too. He was sort of scared, but you were super brave, so he had to be too." With a quick sweeping motion, she picked up her tray and gracefully left the room.

I had to follow her. I wasn't sure why, at first, but I knew I had to. Before she could slip out of sight, I grabbed her free hand, and she turned around. A dizzying flicker of fire shot up my arms and into my head, leaving me momentarily stunned, wondering why I was standing there in the first place.

Charlie looked at me expectantly. "Is he okay?" she finally asked, shattering the silence and gesturing toward the closed curtain we were standing in front of.

"Who? Peter? Oh, yeah. He's fine. He just gets a little green when the needles come out."

"A little? I've seen peas with better coloring." We laughed a little, as I quickly monitored the department. Everyone was doing his or her own thing. Not a soul seemed to care about the moment happening outside of room 6.

"Listen, I just wanted to say thank you." I realized suddenly I was still lightly holding the tip of her index finger. Reluctantly, I pulled my hand away. I didn't want to stop touching her—to break that connection. The energy flowing between us, through so little as a fingertip, was so palpable it was life-breathing. All at once, I was comforted in ways I hadn't been all evening, and it took everything in me to let go.

"Of course. It was nothing." Her gentle features were brushed with subtle humility that looked so appealing on her.

"No. I mean it. You went above and beyond what anyone else has done with her. She really took to you."

"Just doing what they pay me the big bucks for." She smiled again, her magnetic strength keeping my eyes helplessly on hers.

"Hey, Charlie, can you help Ken in 5? I think he needs an EKG," the desk secretary shouted from across the way. Without another word, Charlie sighed and turned away from me once again. I retreated past the closed curtain, left with nothing but the present reality to suck me back down to where I'd been.

❖

Sammy was admitted to a pediatric intensive-care unit in Boston, over an hour away. Peter would ride in the ambulance with her. I would visit in between shifts. This wasn't the first time we'd done this dance, and it wouldn't be the last, by any means. I kissed Sammy's forehead and told her I'd be there to visit the next evening.

"Make sure you eat something" was all Peter could say as he followed the ambulance stretcher out of the building. And once again, I was left alone, standing outside of room 6, looking, I'm sure, almost as disoriented as I felt.

It was four thirty a.m. already, and I was the next morning's six a.m. physician. I hadn't slept in the on-call room since residency, but that night, I just couldn't fathom going home to an empty house. After a quick shower, I changed into a set of fresh scrubs and made my way to the cot in the back of the department in the futile hope of a few minutes of sleep.

No one actually slept in the on-call room, and only a handful of Northwood's elite had the combination to get in—which is why I was startled to be woken up around five thirty a.m. by someone opening the door. A sliver of light poured over my eyes as I quickly covered my face with the crook of my arm.

"What's the matter, Jack? Are you trying to get me up so you can leave early?" I mumbled.

"Oh, my God. Natalie, I'm so sorry...I'm looking for Dr... Well, never mind. I'm just so sorry. I didn't mean to..." Charlie stood with her hand still on the doorknob, looking obviously unnerved as I regained my vision.

"Wait." I stopped her. "It's okay. Don't worry about it."

"I'm really sorry."

"What time is it, anyway?"

She glanced at her wrist. "Five thirty-two."

"Time to get up. Or close enough to it." She still looked embarrassed as she went to leave again. "Hey, come here for a minute."

Charlie hesitated but let go of the knob and walked toward me. I sat up on the cot, hoping she'd sit next to me. She did.

"How do you know so much about SpongeBob?" I tried to contain my amusement as I watched the surprise overwhelm her.

"Okay. I'll fold. I like it." Her eyes shone even in the dim room.

"Clearly. You must have kids, or something. A family?" Could she sense I was beginning to pry? But an enigmatic, ever-growing part of me had to know her. I was curious in a way I'd never been curious about my coworkers or anyone, really— curious in a way I'm sure came across more like nosiness. I didn't care how it looked though. I had to know who she really was.

"Of course I have a family. I wasn't dropped here by aliens last year." I laughed. "No. I have a niece. She's about Sammy's age, actually. My older sister had her when she was eighteen, and I'm pretty much all she's got these days. Her boyfriend's a piece of shit, and our parents retired in Florida when I graduated from medic school. My niece stays with me sometimes, and we watch a lot of SpongeBob."

"What about you? Are you, you know, married?"

"Married? I'm married to this place, I guess. But that's about it."

Something in me I didn't understand felt tremendous relief. I wanted to know more, wanted to know everything there was to know about this baffling twenty-five-year-old who cohabitated my ER. And I wasn't sure why.

"I was in a relationship for a while—a few years—but it didn't work out. She couldn't share me with the job."

Her use of pronouns struck me blind, confirming what I'd already known about her. My father had raised me to believe we were Catholics, but when his drinking swallowed up the rest of his life, he couldn't even keep up the pretext of religion anymore, and we stopped going to Mass. Still, I'd managed to adopt a sort of a-la-carte Christianity, which led me to waver on the standard issues that constantly circulate throughout society without resolution—mainly abortion and homosexuality. I never thought of myself as socially conservative, but being gay was something I'd also never had to deliberate.

"I know how that one goes." I could empathize.

"I don't know," Charlie said, a cunning edge to her voice. "Your husband seems to do all right with it."

"Peter? Oh. Yeah. He does." I was taken aback. I guess I never really placed much emphasis on how Peter felt about my work, or anything, really. Dating had never been a priority to me. While my college classmates were out every weekend with this guy or that, I was inside doing organic-synthesis problems and drinking black coffee. I was twenty-eight when we finally got married. Peter was kind and wanted a couple of children. And I didn't want to be alone forever.

Another knock on the door suddenly stole our attention.

"This is going to start some rumors," she joked under her breath. We both chuckled as Judy opened the door to the on-call room.

"Natalie, it's six…oh…hi, um, Charlie."

"Dear God, can anyone get in this place now?" I laughed.

"Wow, six already, huh? Guess I better head home." Charlie was stammering for some reason.

And with what I thought had to be a swift wink, she shuffled past Judy and was gone.

Chapter Three

The next several weeks brought a schedule that seemed to clash with Charlie's, and I realized I'd been checking the shift board every day to see if she was on. When she was working, I seemed to be consistently conscious of where she was. If I was examining someone in room 4 with a headache, I somehow knew Charlie was in room 3 giving a chest-pain patient nitroglycerine. If I sat at my computer, she often leaned against the nearest desk, shuffling through patient orders, talking to the secretaries, finding ways to keep busy. I was always passively eavesdropping on her conversations. And in my worst moments, I heard myself jumping in, commenting on this or that, just to be involved in whatever was going on around her. Staff, patients, family members—everyone seemed to gravitate toward her.

Maybe it was her charm, or the way she made the nurses laugh with her witty sense of humor. Or maybe it was just her raw intelligence that seeped out of her.

Whatever it was about Charlie, though, I wanted to be a part of it.

❖

A couple of times a year, a few of the nursing staff would find an excuse to throw a department party—which usually just equated to an excuse for everyone to drink beer out of urinals and sing off-key Journey songs to karaoke. It wasn't my ideal way to spend an evening, admittedly, but that particular spring Saturday, I found a sitter for Sammy, picked out a tie for Peter, and put on my only black dress, determined to make the best of what would, essentially, turn into a college frat party.

"Do we have to do this?" Peter groaned, jiggling his tie in the mirror.

"You know we do."

"We've been to a hundred of these things since you finished med school, and every one is exactly the same. Can't you miss just this one?"

"You know I can't."

He signed loudly in protest. "Fine."

"You can stay home with Sammy if you want, Peter. I'm not making you go."

"No, no, of course not." His tone softening, he took a couple of steps toward me and put his hands on my shoulders. "I'm going."

"Okay. Then let me fix this thing." I reached up and pulled at the knot on his tie until I was satisfied it was straight. "There."

"How do I look? Like the husband of a doctor?"

I laughed at him. "Yes. Something like that."

❖

I wondered if she'd be there, as Peter and I made our way to the bar. I wasn't sure why Charlie came to mind, or why she'd been doing it so often over the past several weeks. But I chalked it up to more simple curiosity and took my glass of wine back to the table.

For an hour, Peter and I made small talk with a few of the nurses and administration. Peter got a few miles out of stories about Sammy, and the conversation always ultimately turned to work, until I found myself constantly glancing at the door.

I wasn't at all surprised when Charlie showed up late,

several of the younger nurses greeting her as she arrived, and a few sticking like old chewing gum as she walked confidently to the bar. It was the first time I'd seen her out of uniform, in black pressed dress pants and a royal-blue shirt that hugged her in ways scrubs never could. It wasn't exactly a challenge to see why some of the younger staff fell all over her.

I watched her from the edge of my vision as she slowly sipped a beer and laughed with two of the newly matriculated nurses. They emphasized their age with hair pulled back with matching butterfly barrettes and necklines decorated with cheap silver hearts and stars. Michelle, the older of the two, tossed her long, beautiful hair back behind her shoulder every time Charlie spoke, and the blond nurse scowled when the attention was no longer on her. Periodically, Charlie's eyes would drift in my direction, and I'd panic and turn abruptly to Peter. Once her glass was empty, Charlie placed it on the bar, handed the bartender a ten-dollar bill, and walked, alone, to our table.

"Hi," she said, offering the group a gracious smile. But her eyes rested on me.

"Charlie, hi. Why don't you sit with us?" Everyone at the table nodded in agreement as Judy spoke.

"That's okay. It looks like you're pretty full here. I can sit over…"

"No!" One of the other nurses protested. "We have plenty of room. There's some space next to Natalie. Nat, scoot over." My face warmed like a furnace as I picked my chair up and moved it.

Charlie stood awkwardly, hesitating before beginning to sit down. "Thanks," she said, pulling her chair in and placing her hands nervously on the table in front of her.

"I don't think we've formally met." Peter extended his hand to her. "Peter Anderson."

"Charlie Thompson." She shook it graciously.

"I can't thank you enough for the way you handled Sammy that night."

"Charlie's the best," Judy interjected. "We're lucky to have her."

"You guys are going to make my head explode," she said, her cheeks turning a flattering pink.

❖

It was getting late—with time marked only by the decreasing sobriety of everyone there. Our table was littered with empty beer and wineglasses, and the conversation was becoming sloppy and uncensored. A clearly intoxicated Michelle sauntered up behind Charlie and wrapped her arms around her.

"Come dance with me," she whispered in her ear, probably much louder than she'd realized, and Charlie turned to her.

"I can't dance."

"I'll teach you." Michelle weaved her arm into Charlie's and pulled her up out of her chair. As they both laughed, an unwelcome stitch of jealousy ravaged me.

"Just dance with the girl, will you?" someone yelled, and the two young women took off toward the dance floor.

I watched through hazy vision as Charlie twirled Michelle around and swung her into her arms. She was right; she couldn't dance. But she did it so gracefully, and with so much poise, that no one would have noticed. After several songs, Charlie said something to her I couldn't make out, and Michelle sat down on a nearby bar stool next to the blond nurse.

"Your turn, Natalie," Charlie said, approaching our table again and taking my hands. "That is, if it's okay with Peter."

"Fine with me."

"Thanks, but my dance card's full." I smiled coolly but wondered if anyone was noticing the panic engulfing me. My hands, which still gently held Charlie's, began to shake, and my face flushed for what felt like the hundredth time that night. The thought of even being touched by her was enough to do things to my insides I'd once been sure were nothing more than youthful clichés. And going with Charlie to the dance floor would do nothing but give this reaction away to everyone around me.

"Come on, Nat," Judy said, "lighten up." The table joined in the banter, and I finally resigned my protest, standing slowly and stumbling slightly into Charlie's waiting arms.

The three glasses of wine I'd had kept my apprehension at bay, and as she pulled me a little closer, I could smell the hops on her sweet breath blending with the scent of some kind of expensive cologne. It was strangely comforting and sexy—reasonably reminiscent of the college days I never had. I was dizzy as I spun carelessly, the other partygoers moving lightheartedly around us.

"You really can't dance." I teased her, putting my arms around her neck.

"Told you."

And like an 80's prom-themed movie, the music suddenly slowed, and we were left standing there—her arms tightly holding my waist as we swayed awkwardly to the opening of the new song.

"I, uh, should get back to Peter." I stuttered, looking up into her inviting eyes, which were heavy with an alcohol-enthused lust.

"Thank you for the dance, Miss Jenner," she said with a charming smile, and bowed her head just slightly. I gave a quick mock-curtsey and walked back to my waiting husband.

"Not bad for an old lady," Peter joked, putting his arm around me as I sat back down. "I think some of Charlie's youth wore off on you out there. Charlie, you can't be any more than what, fifteen? sixteen?" He'd just crossed the line into obnoxiously drunk.

"I'm twenty-five," Charlie responded, coldly.

"I met Natalie when I was twenty-five, you know."

"Is that right?" She took another long drag from her beer.

"You should have seen her. She was something back then." Charlie's face contorted with disgust, as she moved protectively closer to me. "I think she's something now," she said with a smug grin, the alpha in her coming to light for the first time since I'd known her, leaving my legs unsteady underneath me.

❖

It was my thirty-ninth birthday, and I was making it a point not to broadcast it to anyone. In one more year, I'd be forty, which, in some obscure way, signified the end of an era of youth to me. The truth, though, was that I hadn't been young a day in my life—save maybe for a few scattered moments like the one with Charlie the month before at the company party. But it was a hospital, a factory of gossip staffed by those with seemingly nothing better to do but talk about one another. And being there as long as I had, someone would, inevitably, find out. I just hoped that someone wouldn't be Charlie. As if it would make some kind of dramatic difference to her whether I was thirty-eight, or thirty-nine, or even forty. As if I should even care how she felt about my age.

And it was, of course, Charlie, who was standing patiently next to my Jeep when I got out of work that day—a sort of palpable eagerness emitting from her.

"What are you doing out here?" I said softly. "Your shift ended hours ago." I crept closer to her, wondering just how close I could get before I felt that same electricity I'd experienced weeks ago. By the time I was near enough to touch her, to smell her, to see the tiny freckles under her cheekbones and the wrinkles around her eyes, I'd lost track of everything.

"I heard it was your birthday."

"Who told you that?" I feigned offense.

"I have my sources. Twenty-nine, right?" She was teasing me.

"Absolutely. I've been twenty-nine for the last ten years, and I plan to stay there indefinitely." We laughed together.

"Turn around." Bewildered, I did what she asked and listened as she fumbled with my passenger-side door. "Okay, you can turn around again."

On the front seat sat a cupcake, with a single candle burning weakly on top of it. "I couldn't let the day go by without doing anything," she said, a hint of uncertainty in her voice as she inspected my face, seeming to assess whether she'd gone too far. Our relationship, our friendship, our status as coworkers was so beyond black and white already. I didn't go home at night and think extensively about anyone else on staff at the hospital. I didn't notice their hair, or their cologne, or their smile, or their laugh. And yet, as far as time spent together went, Charlie and I hadn't had much.

But she hadn't gone too far.

"Happy birthday, Nat," she whispered, and without another thought, I hugged her, wrapping my arms tight around her and planting my face in the warm, sweet skin of her neck, as hot, unexpected tears rushed my eyes.

"Thank you."

"Now," she pulled away from me but never fully released her hold, "blow out this candle before we burn your car down."

❖

The EMS room speaker crackled to life, breaking the peaceful quiet that surrounded the department that afternoon. I'd been catching up on charts for hours and had even had time to eat some lunch that day. This was never a good sign.

"Northwood Hospital, this is Medic 78, code 1." Charlie hurried to the scanner, the boredom in her face quickly dissipating.

"This is Northwood. Go ahead, 78."

"Thirteen-year-old male, near drowning. Fell through the ice at Scutty Pond. He's not breathing. We couldn't get a tube. No IV access. We're bagging him. Pulse is 130, bp is 70 over 45. We'll be there in about two minutes."

And suddenly, the air changed. The growing group around the scanner quickly scattered toward the trauma room, collecting supplies and themselves. Kids were never easy, and they were certainly never fun.

"They couldn't even get the tube?" Charlie snarled from behind me. She was already cracking the pediatric crash cart and drawing up several different medications. "Not even a line? Christ. This kid will be lucky as shit if he gets to us in time." I'd never seen her so worked up. It was like a switch had been flicked inside her and nothing but raw, unfiltered emotion was bubbling out.

"They're here," one of the nurses called from Trauma 10. I quickly followed Charlie into the room.

The small boy was an ominous shade of plum as they moved him to the bed.

"Okay, let's get him tubed. Now." Crushing panic sank in as I realized we probably wouldn't be able to do anything for this boy.

Before I could even move, Charlie was hovering over him, forcefully yet purposefully prying open his mouth. "Someone give me cricoid," she snapped.

As much as the nurses loved Charlie, many of them were intimidated and downright irritated by her skill. She could out-intubate and out-procedure almost every one of them, even the ones who were older than Northwood itself. Still, they knew, we all knew, when things got bad, she could get the job done. I watched, eyes moving back from the flat lines on the monitor to Charlie, as she pushed the tube into the boy's throat.

"I can't see the cords." She pulled the scope back a bit, as I thought about stepping in. "Okay, I've got it." I wanted to cry when the bag began inflating the boy's deprived lungs.

"He's up to ninety-seven percent O2. Good work. Do we have a line yet?" The empowering sense of reprieve didn't last. The young boy was still technically dead.

"Just got one." One of the nurses spoke up. "Pushing

atropine and epi, one milligram." Another nurse continued chest compressions.

"Okay, stop CPR. Let's check the monitor. V-fib. Let's shock him. And push another epi. Also, somebody get the warmer going. We've got to get his temp up. What was it?"

"Ninety, rectally."

"Too cold. Way too cold. Warm him up. And we keep working him. We keep working him until he's warm."

For another several minutes, we pushed drugs and forced air into his body, his small arms flailing wildly as each shock was delivered.

"What's his temp now?"

"Ninety-four," Charlie said emphatically.

"Okay, everybody stop." The tension in the room was thicker than steel, as every individual stepped back to watch the monitors. A slow but clear series of spikes floated across the screen, and the ringing bells of the alarms ceased. "We've got a rhythm."

"And a pulse," Charlie said.

The moment in Trauma 10 seemed to touch everyone.

"Keep warming him up. Two more liters of warm saline, blankets, and watch for more dysrhythmias. Great job. Everyone." And I felt like skipping back to my desk to call for the boy's consult. James Pratt, who fell through the ice on Scutty Pond in late March, would be okay.

❖

Even an hour later, I was still riding the high I got from saving James. To give a kid another seventy, eighty years of life— nothing was better than that. I was on my way to the cafeteria for my third cup of black coffee when I passed the on-call room. Charlie was leaning against the wall nearby, one foot crossed in front of the other, hair tousled in every which direction, a giddy smile on her lips. She was just leaning and smiling. It somehow seemed the most appropriate thing in the world.

"Hey, cowboy," I said, lining myself up next to her, "nice hands in there. Really impressive."

"Me? Are you kidding? Natalie, you saved his life. I've never had a save like that before. I've never...Damn. To have him so close to dead—he was dead—and you just...you stole him back. You knew just what to do. He was dead, and now...he'll go to college, and get married, and maybe have kids, and, Christ, who knows what he'll do now. Because of you."

Charlie looked at me with an admiration, an aching I'd never seen in her before. It was a look that sent every cell in my body tumbling out of control, that caused me to slowly slide in front of the on-call room door, never taking my eyes off her, and punch in the code. With a quick glance down either end of the hallway, I turned the knob as quietly as I could and gripped Charlie's index finger, pulling her gently into the room.

Her admiration appeared to turn to intrigue, but the ache stayed the same. And she never hesitated to follow me.

The room was dark with the door closed—so dark, all I could do was feel her there, in front of me. I could feel the heat emanate from her body. I could feel the worn fabric of her shirt in my fists, feel the short, soft hair on the back of her head as I ran my palms over it.

"Natalie, what are you doing." It wasn't a question but a statement of obligation that we both knew meant nothing at this point.

"I don't know," I said recklessly, "I have no idea what I'm doing. I'm just...doing..."

"You could lose your job...and Peter...and..." She struggled for words, but her fingers moved almost instinctively to the small of my back, gently pulling the hem of my scrub top.

The tension between us was so thick it was painful. My body ached and I writhed to touch her. Something inside me was taking over, something deep and repressed, and neither of us could do anything to stop it.

"Kiss me." I breathed heavily. Instantaneously, I'd become

someone I'd never met before. But I couldn't bring myself to care.

Charlie froze, seeming to probe the darkness for a sign, for anything, that told her this was the right thing to do.

In those minutes, though, right and wrong didn't matter.

I waited. The tumbling speed of everything in me seemed to build, until I felt as if I would self-destruct. I wasn't even sure if that was possible. But it certainly felt like it, while I dared Charlie to close the gap between our lips. I ran my hands over her hard shoulders, down her sides and her hips, and up to her already tousled hair, never taking my eyes off her darkened silhouette.

And then, every bit of energy that had gathered inside of me climbed like bubbles to my head as Charlie grabbed me hard by the shoulders and pulled my lips to hers.

Her fingers were softer than anything I'd ever felt as they moved over my bare skin and up my spine. I pulled my hands through her hair, sinking into the feeling of her lips moving against mine. My legs quivered, and the only thing holding me seemed to be Charlie's body pressed against me.

Nothing else in the world existed but her hands on my waist and her tongue gently brushing my lips. And although my eyes were shut tight, the darkness around me seemed to shift uncontrollably. The world was all at once clearer and more confounding than it had ever been. And a choking fear rose inside me. Nothing would ever be the same again.

CHAPTER FOUR

I came home that night to pork chops, a clean house, and a charming Sammy sitting on the living-room floor, playing with building blocks. Peter was stirring rice pilaf and sipping a glass of red wine. The table was set. National Public Radio was on in the background. Candles lined the runners of the breakfast bar. The room smelled like garlic and potpourri. Nothing was out of place.

"Hi, baby," Peter said with a smile, taking my bag of charts and resting it by the door.

"Hello…" I was still looking around, examining every corner. Where were my fussy Sammy and irritable, haphazard Peter? Where were the cereal ground into the carpet and dirty dishes and overflowing laundry hamper? Before I could contemplate further, Peter leaned forward to kiss me.

"Not now, Peter. I'm sorry. I have to shower. It was a long day."

"Okay. Dinner will be ready when you're out." He smiled again.

I turned the water in the shower up as hot as I could and let it spill over me, attempting to burn whatever it was that left me feeling so empty. Downstairs waited the perfect meal, the perfect family, the perfect house: the perfect life. But I didn't want to leave the hot water. I closed my eyes and let it cascade over my face, seeing Charlie's smile as she leaned against the wall. I saw little James Pratt—imagined him finishing college, becoming a lawyer or a doctor, marrying the girl he loved. I saw the restraint waning in Charlie as she gave in to kissing me, and the same powerful tumbling erupted inside of me until I had to see her. I had to have her again. I braced myself, palms against the shower walls, letting the heat braise my neck. A sort of elated energy I hadn't felt since residency rose in me, from the soles of my feet to my lips, and I felt invincible. I could do anything.

Anything, except go back downstairs.

Sammy was on the couch, wedged between Peter and the arm of the sofa, giggling uncontrollably as he read *Tinker Bell* to her for what was probably the fifth time that night. Dinner was on the table. The smell of thawing early spring air was creeping in through a propped-open window in the entryway. Everything surrounding me was inarguably faultless. Everything inside me felt wrong.

I kissed Sammy on her forehead and sat beside her on the couch, pulling her as close to me as I could. "Hi, honey," I said, and she looked at me, smiled a wide, crooked smile, and kissed me back.

Peter remained next to her still, with a face that reminded me of a lap dog needing to be coddled. Impatiently, he leaned toward me again, and without another excuse to offer, I allowed him to get up and kiss me. The stark contradiction between his mouth and my earlier afternoon in the call room shook me, reminded me of the beginning of a dark tunnel with no way out. Panic seeped into my body, through my lips, into my skin, until it crawled on every inch of me. And as Peter tried to wake up whatever in me was dormant, or dead, in regard to him, I counted the seconds until I could pull away.

"I'm starving." I broke contact. "Let's eat. I bet Sammy's hungry too." I stood up from the couch and swung her up into my arms, pecking her cheeks and her forehead as she laughed uncontrollably. "I missed you today, honey. Did you have a good time with Daddy?" She pulled curiously at the loose strands of hair running down my shoulders and nodded. "Did you play… detectives?" She nodded again, this time more emphatically.

"We went to the grocery store too, didn't we, Sam? And…we went to the TOY STORE!" She nodded again. "Show Mommy what you got."

Sammy squirmed out of my grip and ran to the chair in the corner of the room, picking up a brand-new Barbie doll.

"That's nice, sweetie. Peter," I snapped, turning to him, "you can't go buying her something just to keep her happy. We've been over this."

"It's just a doll, Nat. It's ten dollars."

"That's not the point. You can't buy her affection!"

Peter sat down at the table and started cutting up Sammy's pork chops. "No, Natalie. The point is that you don't want me spending your money."

"Oh, is that it?" I whispered harshly. "So now I'm selfish? I work every goddamn day for this family. I'm the reason we have a meal to eat tonight! I'm the reason we can afford to pay for Sammy to have nice things."

"And I'm just Mr. Natalie Jenner. Right? Stay-at-home dad. Unemployed. Scum of the earth. Spends all his wife's hard-earned cash while she's out saving lives all day. That's it, isn't it, Nat?"

Before I had a chance to rebut, Sammy began to cry—the usual marker to the end of our blowouts. We sat through the rest of dinner in silence until I took the stairs back to my study to surf endless journal articles, where I would, eventually, fall asleep.

❖

By the time the six a.m. sunlight poked through the office blinds, I was already awake, staring blankly at my computer screen saver, trying to remember when I'd dozed off. The hospital wasn't expecting me until noon, but I couldn't stay in the house with Peter. I was still angry about the previous night's accusations, but more than that, I just couldn't seem to stomach another minute inside my own head.

It was warming up nicely outside by the time I headed out the door. The driver's-side window to my Jeep was rolled down partway, and the April air was rushing in over my head. Everything about the day held promise for change and optimism. Birds were singing from the roofs of nearby houses, and baggy-jeaned teenagers were skateboarding down the street.

As I pulled into the parking lot in front of the Northwood Emergency Department, I thought about Charlie again, although she'd been the ever-present image in my mind for days now. Was she inside those doors? Would I walk in and see her standing by the nurses' station, or pass her calming a patient's family member in one of the exam rooms? Would I get to see her smile at me, hear her say my name, feel her brush my arm, only somewhat unintentionally, as she passed by?

But then, as I approached the automatic doors to the waiting area, I forced a new thought into my wobbling head that said I couldn't be thinking those other thoughts, that I was a doctor first and couldn't get involved in the personal lives of my coworkers. I was a mother second and couldn't leave my only child in any way. I was a wife. I'd made vows and commitments, and had obligations and financial ties, and a child, and a dog, and a house, and a reputation…and a friend—a friend I'd known and shared my life with for a decade now.

And then came the thought that I had a reputation to uphold, as a physician, a mother, a wife—a member of society. I wasn't that woman who kissed other women in dark rooms. I couldn't be that woman.

Charlie was the first face I saw inside. She stood at the window to the triage area, chart in hand, speaking softly with one of the nurses, about what I wasn't sure. As I passed by quickly, I wondered if she'd notice when I didn't say hello—or even when

I refused to make eye contact. I didn't want to hurt her, but I couldn't look at her either.

The department was small, and avoiding someone wouldn't be easy. For the first couple of hours, I managed to stay at my desk, working on charts, only getting up to see patients. On the occasions when our paths crossed in the halls, I would feign looking at my watch, patient notes, my cell phone, or anything else I could to appear distracted.

My extensive training had allowed me to maintain focus only on the medicine, when it was required. But the moment I let my guard slip and the medicine be put aside, there was Charlie again, in my thoughts, under my skin, and sometimes in my line of sight. In the moments when she would appear in front of me, I would allow myself a glance, taking in her eyes, her lips, and then, I would begin to remember how she felt, how she smelled, and I forced myself to disengage.

By the sixth hour, Charlie began to hover near my chair— picking up charts, shuffling through them and putting them down, talking to anyone around, finding reasons to pass by whenever she could. It wouldn't be possible to escape confrontation.

"Natalie." She spoke quietly, in a manner that was completely juxtaposed to her normal persona. "Can you take a look at this EKG for me?"

"Yeah. Sure. Okay. Uh. What's the story?" As she handed me the piece of paper, her fingers brushed my wrists, and heat blistered up my arms, warming me to the core.

"Fifty-four years old, no history, came in with chest pain for two days radiating to the back. I wasn't sure about those flips there…"

"Looks okay," I said, unthinkingly looking up into timid green eyes that had never looked so unsure. "Keep him monitored, but I'd say as long as the lab work is okay he can go home." As long as I didn't look at her, I was okay.

Without another word, she picked up the EKG and turned

away. "Okay," she whispered aggressively, turning back toward me again, "you've been avoiding me like the Ebola virus all day. What the hell is going on?" The anger in her voice wasn't as disturbing as the desperation.

"I can't talk about this right now, Charlie. I'm working."

"Fine. Then come to the employee lounge."

I paused for a minute, thinking about the piles of paperwork that were building up at my desk and, again, about what people would think if they saw us whispering by the microwave. But then, I erroneously looked at her again, and the softness in the lines of her young face, the sharp curves of her worked hands, the subtle wrinkles at the corners of her eyes crushed me like a wrecking ball. I was defenseless.

"Okay. Meet me in there in five minutes."

I finished writing up room 5's prescriptions, wondering all the while how I would tell Charlie I could never let what happened the day before happen again—how I would ever convince her I didn't want it to happen again.

Charlie was already waiting for me, sitting at the table, rhythmically bouncing her leg up and down to an impatient song inside her head.

"I don't have much time, Charlie. What did you need to talk to me about?"

"Really? You don't know?" Her tone was brash, in a way that reminded me of the day James Pratt almost died on her watch.

"Look, Charlie—"

"You don't have to say it. I've heard it before. You're not the first straight woman I've been with. And you're not the first one who's given me this speech either." I felt my face fall in surprise. Until that moment, I'd never really allowed myself to think of the women Charlie had pined over in the past—or worse, the ones she would undoubtedly pine over in the future. "You're going to tell me that you're married—that you're not gay. And that what happened with us," she swallowed loudly and choked back her words, "can never happen again."

I could do nothing but nod absently.

"I get it. Really. I do. And believe me, I don't hold it against you."

"You don't?"

"Of course I don't. These things happen all the time. You have a lot of shit to deal with, between Sammy, and Peter, and this job. It's easy to get confused." Her empathetic undertones made her that much more appealing, until the short distance between our two chairs seemed almost unbearable.

"It is? Yeah. Confused. Right." I found myself involuntarily leaning closer to her.

"But we still have to work together. I have to feel like I can come to you about patients, or whatever else, and you aren't going to avoid me."

"Right…of course…" I said sharply, recoiling into myself. This wasn't how I'd anticipated our meeting going. I'd prepared for tears. I'd prepared for yelling. I'd prepared for everything… except tolerance. Of course Charlie would take rejection better than any woman on earth. Of course she would walk out of the room, never looking back, swing in her step, making me crave her more than I ever thought possible.

❖

Weeks passed, weeks when I was forced to drown myself in paperwork, and research, and patients, and trauma, and death, and, if I was lucky, preventing death. Weeks when I did everything I could to forget about the young paramedic who seemed to be disrupting my every moment of rational thought. Peter noticed. I'm sure of it. The distance I'd placed between us was as subtle as a bullet wound, as I remained in my study, or occupied my time with Sammy, whenever I was home.

The hospital used to infatuate me, but like an old lover, it became comfortable and almost listless without the intrigue of a moment with Charlie. I still enjoyed my work, of course—that was inevitable. But, much to my chagrin, some of my passion was gone. Maybe I was just getting old. Or maybe the burning need I'd always transposed to the emergency room had finally met its match—and nothing quite satisfied it anymore.

I lay awake at night agonizing over what should have been nothing more than a simple kiss. I wasn't exactly prom queen, but I wasn't completely immune to the charms of a first kiss either.

So why was this one so different? Why did I insist on playing it over and over in my head, whenever I could, like some immaculate daydream? Why did my body react so fiercely to the memory, causing me to ache to relive it? It had been, after all, nothing more than an irrational, elated reaction to an intense situation.

Saving a life is sort of like being drunk. Judgment takes a backseat to passion, and passive thoughts become acute actions. I've seen people scream, cry, sing, dance, even hit each other in the moments following an anxious moment in the ER. So why was a kiss so unreasonable? I was attracted to the ease and grace with which Charlie was able to treat James, and that was as far as the attraction could go.

Chapter Five

It was early in the evening, and I was preparing for a long night, as I always did when working the late shift. Often, it was quiet enough. But I could never be sure what to expect. And when the rest of the world was asleep, everything felt a little more urgent.

"Got one on the flight deck for you, Natalie," Michelle, the same young night nurse from the party, with the big, red lips and a body that belonged in magazines, said cheerfully.

With a diminished degree of interest, I reached up to the rack and pulled out the chart, eyes still stuck to a previous patient's CAT scan. Michelle and one of the other nurses stood watching, small smiles lingering on their faces.

"What? Is it the president or something?"

"Not quite, no," Michelle said quietly, suppressing a childish giggle.

I glanced quickly at the chart—26, female, abdominal pain for a day, fever, nausea, vomiting.

"Okay. A belly pain. What am I missing here? What's so funny?"

The girls glanced at each other. "Just take a look at the name."

Hazy, and slightly irritated by the charades, I allowed my eyes to scan to the top of the page, where the patient's demographics sat—a part I usually skipped over until just before entering the exam room. There it was—Thompson, CarolAnne.

"Charlie…" I mumbled, more to myself than either nurse.

"Looks like our big, bad resident paramedic is down for the count," Michelle said with a wink. "I'll get labs started…" She took off quickly.

"Michelle. Be nice. Please?"

I collected myself before entering room 5, unconsciously smoothing stray strands of my hair and adjusting the neckline of my scrub top. Skimming the notes, I thought about what this would mean. For weeks, I'd managed to keep Charlie at a proper distance, approaching her about patients and smiling when I passed her in the hall, all the while avoiding dark call rooms and any situation that might threaten my control.

Now, I faced another kind of situation. Charlie was the patient and I was the doctor. I didn't have anyone else to pass her off to, in order to protect my professional and physical boundaries, and even if I had, refusing to treat her would certainly raise an eyebrow or two among the staff. It was bad enough I lived amongst a constant backdrop of paranoia, wondering if anyone knew the events of the month before.

This is your job.

Chart in tow, I reminded myself to put one foot in front of the other, eyes straight ahead, although my heart erupted at a dizzying rate the closer I got to her room.

"I swear I didn't know you were on tonight. If I had I would have tried to hold off a little…" Charlie said with a contrived smile.

"Stop it. How bad is it?" Even in a drab hospital gown she looked painfully attractive. The muscles in my stomach tightened quickly as I realized I was staring.

"Oh, not too bad. Just a little pain in my lower right quadrant. Started this afternoon…"

"You're a terrible liar. Just awful. The heroic paramedic would not have come to her own ER for 'just a little pain.' Now lie back," I said, surprised by the insistent tinge in my voice.

"Anything you want." An arresting and overtly seductive

smile framed by flushed cheeks rose on her lips. I froze, unable to physically pull myself away from her stare and to the side of her bed for the exam. My mouth hung slack-jawed, silence filling the small space. "I'm sorry…I…That was…"

"Not cool."

"Not cool at all." But I couldn't help notice the amused grin Charlie tried to contain.

I hesitated, watching her stretch out on her back, noting the thin layer of cotton that lay between where my hands needed to be and her strong body. And for the first time since residency, I wasn't sure I could do this.

"I wouldn't have come in…but, you know…right lower quadrant…I still have my appendix…for now."

Charlie's suddenly professional demeanor strengthened my resolve. "I'll get you some Dilaudid. We'll have to see what your lab work says, but I'm glad you came in." Heat rose up my neck at the sincerity of my own words. "Does this hurt?" I said sternly, taking a deep breath and pushing gently on the area just beneath her ribs. The muscles beneath my hands quivered for a moment as I touched her, and I could feel the fever working its way through her body.

"No, not there."

I moved my hands lower, resting my palms on the V-shaped curves of her stomach, softly pressing down, lingering longer than I probably should have, as Charlie sucked in a ragged breath.

"I thought you said it was the right side?" I asked, perplexed.

"I did…" My resolve waned, my own breath catching in my throat, a sudden wave of fire crashing over my entire body. It was amateurish and absurd to lose control with patients—something I hadn't done for years, and never like this, but something I seemed to be doing that night, with my patient in room 5.

I cleared my suddenly parched throat, trying to dismantle the fog that had settled over my vision. "Okay. Any nausea?" I said, stoically, pressing somewhat harder now into the hollow just above Charlie's pelvic bone. A small tattoo curled up her side and crept toward her belly button, creating what resembled shadows on her level stomach. Her skin was pale from a Rhode Island winter and as smooth as I remembered. Abruptly, I found myself wishing I'd put gloves on. She was soft, and warm. And as she winced slightly under my touch, I realized she was vulnerable too.

"A little," she said.

"You're clearly tender there."

"Thanks, Doc. Glad you went to medical school for that."

"Glad to know you're a smart-ass even when you're sick."

Charlie slowly released a heartbreaking smile, slightly less practiced than others of hers I'd seen. Her eyes glistened with pain and maybe even a dash of fear. Her broad shoulders leaned carefully against the head of the bed, the thin gown hugging her just below her defined collarbones and falling freely. Another tattoo I'd noticed many times before eclipsed her right forearm, accentuating the lines that ran adjacent to gently toned muscle.

Hardly topping five feet three, Charlie always felt much taller than that to me. But lying in the hospital bed in room 5, she appeared delicate, and breakable—in need of saving. It could have been her youth, bundled with the image of defenselessness, that forced me to fight the impending urge to sit next to her and hold her. To stroke her hair, comfort her, fix her. Or maybe it was just the innate part of me I'd never been able to cure, the part that drew me to what needed to be saved.

"It's appendicitis, isn't it?" Her voice sounded suddenly grave and fierce.

"I'm not sure yet. We have to get your labs back. And then, a CT…and…"

"Just tell me, Natalie."

I took in a deep breath and sat down in the small alcove of space left by Charlie, turning to look at her blunted, beautiful eyes. "I don't know. You know I don't know yet. But it's likely.

Yes." She ran a hand through her hair, and I wanted more than anything to reach out and touch her.

"Okay..." she breathed again, "okay. I can handle that. Okay."

If I sat by her another second, I'd finger the hair on the back of her neck and pull her into me, like I did that afternoon that felt like so many happy lifetimes ago. Wrong time, I told myself. Wrong time. Wrong place. Wrong person. Wrong gender.

I got up to leave without another word.

"Nat?" she said quietly, a hint of need in her voice so palpable I turned from the door to make sure she was all right.

"Yes?"

"You'll be here...right?"

I smiled, struck by the earnestness of her words. This was the first time I'd seen Charlie exposed, without the cover of the job to cloak herself in. It was the first time I'd felt she was really, truly unsure. It was stunning. "Right here...Every step. I promise."

I wanted to stay with her, to erase the fear I saw her trying desperately to hide. But the ever-growing stack of patient charts was glaring at me from my desk, and it was getting late. Besides, I couldn't do any more for Charlie. We would need to see the lab results.

The night was busier than most, and I tried futilely to get to the others who needed me. I read through the notes of the five-year-old with nausea and vomiting in room 2, and then, when I realized I hadn't absorbed a word, I read them again, and again. On my third or fourth go-around, I was stopped mid-sentence by the sound of laughter coming from down the hall—Charlie's laughter.

The curtain to her room was cracked open just enough to allow me, and everyone who passed by, to see the young, beautiful Michelle sitting next to her bed, chair pulled up so close she could rest her hands next to Charlie's. As I watched, Michelle would smile at her, listening to her stories with unbreakable interest.

Every now and then, Charlie's face would harden slightly, and her eyes would linger on the floor, and Michelle would reach up a manicured hand and stroke Charlie's wild hair.

A burst of sickening heat erupted in me as I watched Michelle touch her, and my churning stomach lurched hard into my chest. With a deep breath, I turned back to the work in front of me.

As soon as I felt it was reasonable, I checked for Charlie's lab results, half of me wanting to treat her and the other half frantically seeking an excuse to interrupt whatever was going on between the two of them.

❖

"Charlie," I said, eyes locked on her chart as I entered the room. I felt her look up at me, breaking her hold on the pretty nurse seated by her side. "I have your labs back."

I glared at Michelle, furiously willing her to leave the room, to leave me alone with Charlie. Instead, she remained seated, leaning even closer, until her breasts nearly brushed Charlie's shoulder, daring me with abrasive blue eyes to challenge her. What was I doing? Charlie wasn't mine to have, or to even have any say in who she flirted with, or, I thought, fighting a sudden wave of nausea, slept with.

"Michelle…I need a rectal temp on the little boy in room 2." She stared at me for a moment, a glimmer of pure hatred in her eyes, and proceeded out the door. For an unfocused second, I wondered if Michelle, who'd always seemed to like me well enough, was angry with me because she wanted Charlie…or because she thought I did too…

"Sorry…she was just…we were…" Charlie said.

"No. No, stop right there." I held out my hand. "I don't want to know."

"Really. It's not like that. She's just a friend…A good friend."

"It looked like a little more than that," I said, the bitterness in my words seeping out far more than I'd hoped.

"Okay. She's tried, a couple of times. On the Saturdays when I work day shift, some of us go to Shooters for drinks. At times, Michelle will have too much, and she'll…try to take me home."

The same familiar lurching in my belly came on so strongly I grew light-headed.

"I didn't know Michelle was…"

"I don't think she does either…But after a few drinks, you'd be amazed what people will try to pawn off on the booze."

"I see…well, you don't owe me any explanation."

"I know." She furrowed her brow slightly, and the features on her perfect face softened brilliantly. "But somehow, I feel like I do."

A beat of uncomfortable silence filled in between us as images of a drunken Michelle running her hands up Charlie's thigh flooded into my head.

"So, my labs?" she said seriously, snapping me out of my adolescent envy.

"You have a bit of a white count—"

"How high?"

"Twenty-two—"

"That's more than 'a bit,' Nat. Appendicitis is looking more like it every minute, huh?" She chewed nervously on her bottom lip until it was swollen and pink.

"You pretty much diagnosed yourself the moment you walked in here. But we can't know for sure. We still have to do a CT."

"But it's pretty likely."

I nodded. "Given your fevers, your pain, and the white count."

"Thank you for being honest with me." She smiled a small smile my way.

"It's hard to put much past you, Charlie."

The space between us seemed to ignite, and I once again fought the unyielding desire to touch her, to be close to her. I just wanted to comfort her. That was all. I wanted to fix her.

"Listen, you know I hate to be like this, but I'm still pretty uncomfortable..."

"I'll get you another milligram of Dilaudid," I said tenderly.

"Thank you."

❖

Half an hour later, I passed her room again, wondering if I could find an excuse to step inside. Without one in mind, I found myself opening the curtain the rest of the way to reveal Charlie curled up on her side, sound asleep. One arm was tucked under her head, and her eyes fluttered softly under closed lids. I hated waking her but knew if any of the nurses had seen just how long I'd been standing there watching her, I'd have to.

"Charlie..." I whispered, sitting in the chair Michelle had occupied and gently rubbing her shoulder. "Charlie...wake up..." Her body felt like crushed velvet under my hands, as I temporarily lost track of time and surroundings.

A quick, throaty moan escaped her lips, and she turned slowly onto her back to face me. "Now there's a way to wake up," she said softly, her eyes bright, with tiny specs for pupils looking back at me. My cheeks and neck flushed violently, and I was grateful for the darkness around us.

"How's your pain now?"

"Not a problem at all," she said lightly.

"Good. Well, then I'll be back after your CAT scan with the final word." As I approached the doorway, I ached with a question I hadn't yet asked, one that had nothing to do with pain levels or medications or allergies. It would be highly inappropriate to take advantage of the state the narcotics had left her in. But, as was often the case around Charlie, logic gave way to inherent need.

"Let me ask you something," I said as Charlie sat up, squinting her eyes into focus.

"Anything."

"Michelle…when you went out to Shooters and she…well, did you…"

"Did I sleep with her? That's what you want to know, isn't it?" Her face lit up with obnoxious, boastful pride that was somehow so endearing on her.

"Yes…"

"No. No. I've never slept with her. Not even once."

I found myself bathed in a sense of relief I felt only when I saved a life, one that disturbed me when out of context.

"How come? I mean, look at her. She's a freaking supermodel."

"She's no Natalie Jenner…" Charlie's voice, husky with fatigue, sent waves of fitful need over my body. And as I stood wordlessly, she drifted back to sleep, a smile still resting on her lips.

❖

A CAT scan confirmed what we'd all suspected—Charlie had acute appendicitis. Even the most minor of surgeries wouldn't be easy for someone as tough and stubborn as she was. People like Charlie were the best kind of people but the worst kind of patient.

"It's appendicitis, isn't it," Charlie stated the moment I walked in the room. I wasn't sure if I was really that transparent around her or if her own intuition was just that finely tuned. Either way, I didn't seem to be able to hide anything from her.

"Yes. It's pretty inflamed."

"Damn…"

After a moment, I allowed myself to cross the room and, once again, sit by her side. "It's not a big deal. You know that. You're healthy and young."

"I'm not that young!" she cut in, defensively.

"Well, you're not older than dirt, like I am."

"You're not that old, Nat."

"I could have a kid your age…"

"Yeah, if you started trying at twelve. We have twelve years and ten months between us…That's nothing," she said, sweetly.

"Charlie, what were you doing in '85?"

She thought for a moment, bringing her hand to her chin. "I wasn't doing much of anything. But my parents were contemplating having a bright, devastatingly good-looking little girl who'd grow up to be the best medic Northwood has ever seen." Her grin was so wide it appeared to take over her entire face.

"Please. You've had too much Dilaudid." Charlie laughed at me, then feigned offense. "No, but really, do you know where I was in 1985? I was in junior high, hanging out here, sneaking glances at patients' charts when my father wasn't looking. I was here…and you weren't even born yet. You want to talk about older than dirt…"

And for the first time, the years between us felt like lifetimes. Charlie was young, now only twenty-six, with her best years still far ahead of her. She was young and heart-stoppingly gorgeous in a way that caused me to think in clichés and daydream like a teenager. She was bright as hell—any medical school would be lucky to take her. She lived fast, and hard, and she could charm her way out of any situation and into anyone's bed—except mine, that was. Yes. Charlie had everything to live for and everything to offer someone. Why she insisted on focusing her attention on me all seemed far too mystifying.

"Older is sexy." She reached out a hand toward my cheek.

"Charlie, stop…" I reluctantly intercepted it.

"Sorry…It's the Dilaudid, really…" But this time, she wasn't smiling.

I pulled back farther, allowing for an uncomfortable amount

of space between us, contemplating what I could possibly say to rectify the hurt I'd just put on Charlie's face.

"Dr. Jacobs will be over to see you in the morning. In the meantime, we'll move you to a real room upstairs." She nodded solemnly. "You'll be just fine. No big deal." I got up and left the room.

"Natalie." I heard Charlie call my name, even after I'd already stepped into the hall. I poked my head back through the curtain. "Will you visit?"

Once again taken aback by the susceptibility in her tone, I froze. There was no harm in visiting a patient...was there? No one would find that out of place.

"Of course I will..." And I once again left the room, feeling her eyes work me over as I did.

❖

Charlie was moved to a room on the second floor sometime around four a.m. It wasn't expected or even normal for the physician to accompany a patient to their room—especially for a simple case of appendicitis. But I couldn't steer my tired mind away from Charlie's pleas for me to stay with her—to visit. Her parents were in Florida, and her sister was at home with her kids. I could have asked Michelle to escort her, but every time I considered it, my stomach turned. She was my patient.

"You ready to go?" I asked, walking into her room.

Charlie's eyes opened wide and her entire face brightened up the dark room.

"Really? You're going with me?"

Her enthusiasm thrilled me. "Sure. We're pretty empty. Just you and the drunk down the hall sleeping it off. Besides, if something happens, they can beep me."

"Not like it's a big place," she teased me. I pulled her bed away from the wall and began to push her toward the elevator.

❖

"Careful. You've had a lot of meds," I said, helping her up off the stretcher and slipping my arm around her waist as she leaned on me.

"You just want an excuse to touch me." She paused for a moment, gauging my reaction. When I finally allowed a minute smirk to peek from my lips, she leaned closer to me, her mouth nearly touching my ear. "It's okay, I'm not complaining."

I shivered hard as the wanting in her words warmed my skin.

A figure appearing in the doorway rocked me hastily away from my trance.

"CarolAnne? I'm Joe. I'll be your nurse for the rest of the morning."

Charlie smiled weakly at the man in the green scrubs, a look of anguish seeping onto her face as she sat on the bed. "Charlie. Call me Charlie."

"Okay, Charlie. And you're…her nurse?"

My gaze stayed glued to Charlie, and it was several more seconds before I realized the young man was speaking to me. "Me? Oh. No. I'm her…I'm with…Dr. Jenner. From the ER?"

Joe's big brown eyes grew even larger as he struggled to find words. "Dr. Jenner…I'm so sorry. I only work nights here, and I haven't seen…I'm not used to doctors bringing…I was just…"

"It's okay. Honestly. This is pretty unorthodox, I suppose." I allowed Charlie my coyest smile, and for a beautiful moment, color flooded back into her cheeks, and her hollow dimples poked out from above soft, potent lips.

"Well, anyway," Joe said, and I wondered if he felt some of the same exquisite tension I did. "I'm sorry, Dr. Jenner, but I need to get Charlie situated here."

"Just give me a minute with her, okay?"

Charlie and Joe exchanged puzzled glances, but neither dared question my request. Without argument, Joe left the room, and Charlie and I were once again alone.

"Listen," I said in a hushed voice, sidling up next to the bed Charlie was occupying and stroking the wild strands of her hair that fell onto the white pillow. "You're going to be fine. Really."

"Thanks—for all of this, Natalie. I mean it." She grabbed my hand and held it tight next to her face. "I guess you are more than just a good doctor."

"Very funny. I'll check in on you, okay?"

"Will you visit me? When I get out, I mean?" My heart sank almost audibly inside my chest, and I was left feeling hollow and disgusted.

That wasn't going to happen. I couldn't find a way to explain to Peter I'd be at the hospital again in a few hours or to explain to the staff on the surgical floor why I was spending so much time with a paramedic who worked with me. People would talk. Peter would suspect something wasn't right. And a little distance from Charlie felt all too necessary.

"No, it's okay. I know you're busy. I'm sorry I asked...I don't know what I was thinking..."

Her humility was heartbreaking and, in ways I couldn't fully comprehend, unconventionally sexy.

"I'll try."

After a beat more of what was surely disappointment, Charlie reached toward her neck and began removing the medallion around it. "Would you mind?" she asked casually, handing me the necklace. "I can't wear it into surgery."

"No. Of course not."

"It's St. Jude." She must have noticed me keenly studying the lusterless metal in my hand. "It was my grandfather's."

"I didn't know you were Catholic."

"Hardly. But he was. He was a surgeon, and before that, he was a corpsman in the navy, and a firefighter. Kind of an all-around American hero…Mine, at least…" Charlie's clouded eyes smiled at the memory, and I nodded back tenderly.

"Sounds like you haven't followed far from his footsteps…" And what would normally have been a pristine opportunity for Charlie to boast, or flirt, or overproduce confidence passed with nothing more than reflective silence. "I'll keep it safe," I said, closing my hand around the jewelry.

"I know you will. And besides, it gives you a reason to have to see me again."

"Charlie…we work together…"

"Maybe one day when we're not working…" My eyes betrayed me, and Charlie's light features suddenly fell. "Relax, Doc. I know. We can't. You can't. You aren't. You don't…want to. I know."

I squeezed her hand one last time, still stinging from the last few words she'd said, and quietly walked away.

❖

Staying at the hospital wouldn't bring Charlie out of surgery any faster, and working late was doing nothing to ease the anxiety and lingering sadness I sat engulfed with. I tapped quickly on the surface of my desk and flicked my eyes back and forth from chart to chart, until I finally decided home, with my daughter, was the best place for me to be. Besides, I'd worked all night. Sleep would do me good, although I had a feeling it wouldn't come easily.

It was nine a.m. by the time I arrived home. Peter, who'd begun doing contracting work for a friend's electrical repair business, was already gone, and I couldn't help but feel relief at not having to force fervor in his presence. Sammy was in the den, watching cartoons with the nanny.

"Hi, sweetie," I said, reaching down to coddle Sammy in my arms. "I missed you so much…" Sammy giggled a little at the television and, with only mild interest, hugged my neck. "Thanks for coming over, Becka." Our nanny, who we'd only recently hired due to Peter finally going back to work, had agreed to take Sammy for a few hours in the morning so I could sleep when I worked nights.

"No problem, Dr. Jenner. She's a doll. Like always."

"Stop with that doctor crap. Natalie is just fine."

"Will do. Now why don't you go upstairs and get some sleep? Sammy and I are good down here for a while."

"Thank you."

I once again ascended the stairs to our bedroom, rejuvenated by the sight of my perfect, smiling child. But the heat of the shower, the softness of the bedding, the stream of sunlight flowing in through the window offered no reprieve. Charlie's pale, sickly face was all I could see. I lay sleeplessly caressing the St. Jude medallion that rested on my chest. And soon a neurotic checking of the clock, with me fruitlessly wondering whether Charlie was out of the OR yet, replaced sleep. Was she all right? And then, just as fatigue finally began to win out, a new thought jolted me awake: Charlie would wake up alone. I should have been there.

It was three p.m. when I finally gave up the idea of rest, put on a lavender button-up shirt and jeans, and raced back downstairs.

"Becka," I called into the den. "Becka? Sammy?"

The two emerged from the kitchen, red sauce covering Sammy's cheeks as she stood holding Becka's hand. "What is it? Is everything okay?"

"Yes. Everything's fine. But do you think you could watch Sammy for a few more hours? I have to follow up on a patient."

"Well, sure, but…I didn't think emergency-room doctors followed their patients like…"

"It's a…um…special situation."

Becka nodded, seemingly aware she was delving too deeply into something personal. "Of course."

"Great," I said, pecking Sammy on the top of her head and simultaneously grabbing my car keys off the table by the door. "Peter will be home around six. Make sure he pays you. I love you, Sammy Girl."

❖

I was back at the hospital, taking the stairs to Charlie's room, before even beginning to realize what I was doing. It seemed like the most logical thing in the world to be there with Charlie when she was alone. No one should come out of anesthesia by themselves. She was a friend, and she needed someone. All other accompanying thoughts and agendas had to remain buried.

"Good afternoon, Dr. Jenner." The desk clerk greeted me as I approached.

"Hi there." I lowered my voice. "I'm looking for Charlie Thompson. Is she out of surgery yet?"

The woman stared at me in a way that led me to believe she would, without doubt, be circulating some fragment of gossip surrounding me. When I refused to give her anything more to work with, she flipped through a laminated booklet next to her and ran a long fingernail down a freshly printed page.

"Charlie is back. She's in her room now. Has been for a while, actually. Would you like to see her chart, Doctor?" She sounded patronizing.

"No…no, that won't be necessary, thanks."

"So this is personal?" Her excitement was brimming over her bifocals. It was clear now that this was the kind of secretary who thrived on hospital drama, and physician drama was the jackpot.

"Thank you for your help." I left her with a tight-lipped smile and headed down the hall to Charlie's room.

I didn't get an answer when I knocked on her door, but somehow I opened it anyway. I found her in bed, arms resting on her stomach, with Court TV on low in the background. Her eyes were closed, and a soft snore escaped her mouth. She looked so wonderful sleeping—the very definition of young, untouched beauty. It was the image of someone who'd never had a struggle in life, someone I knew wasn't Charlie. But it was nice to witness, nonetheless.

As I watched her from the doorway, the need that made me hurt to climb into bed next to her and just feel her beside me frightened me. I wanted to pull her arms around me and wrap myself in her until every confusing emotion I had was contained. Or, at least, until I didn't care anymore.

Instead, I settled for standing in the doorway, gazing at the rhythmic, symmetrical rise and fall of her chest as she breathed.

I'm not sure how long I was in the doorway before her eyes fluttered open and she lifted her head. "Hey," she said in a deep, scratchy alto. "How long have you been there?"

"Oh…just a minute." Did she know I was lying, that I'd lost complete and utter track of time watching her dream? How elated would she be if she knew that?

"I can't believe you made it. I didn't think you would…"

"Sammy's got a sitter, and Peter's at work. I couldn't sleep so I thought I'd come in and get some work done." I studied her face as she tried to mimic my pathetic attempt at nonchalance.

"Sit with me. Please. I was just catching up on my *Judge Judy*."

I pulled up a chair next to the head of the bed. "I wanted to get this back to you right away." I carefully slid the necklace from around my neck and placed it around Charlie's.

"You wore it—"

"Yeah. I hope that's okay."

"Of course it's okay," she said with a charmed smile.

"How are you feeling?"

She gestured to the IV pump humming next to her. "They're keeping me comfortable."

"Are you sure? Because if you're not, I can get you orders written for morphine, or more Dilaudid, or—"

"Nat, that's sweet. But I'm fine. Really. And besides, do you really have the authority to do that up here?"

"Oh, I have all sorts of authority you don't know about."

A suggestive smirk quirked her pale lips, and her eyes sparkled. "Oh, really?"

"That's not how I meant!" I protested, but the cherry of my cheeks said otherwise. I never intended to mislead her, to be that woman who loves being pursued. But the words that snuck out of my mouth around her often sounded flirtatious and unfamiliar. This wasn't me. I was safe, and controlled. And nothing about this situation was.

CHAPTER SIX

Charlie was going to be out of work for two weeks recovering, while I submerged myself in my patients with a sort of monotony I couldn't really fathom. Nothing felt the same without her.

"Has anyone heard from Charlie?" someone would say, and my heart would explode. A nervousness I hadn't felt since my first day of medical school would slowly build in me, until I wanted to run, or scream, or cry. But I couldn't. So I'd bury myself in whatever work I could find, trying to put Charlie as far to the back of my mind as she would possibly go.

No one mentioned the fact I'd been the one to stay with her the day she came out of surgery. Maybe no one knew. Or, if they did, they probably didn't find it all that unusual. What was unusual, though, was what I was feeling without her.

❖

"I was thinking we could go out this weekend," Peter said softly, climbing under the covers of our king-sized bed.

"Go out?" I didn't hide my surprise well.

"Yes. You know, on a date?"

"Peter, we haven't dated since…Christ, we've never dated."

"So? I want to start." He turned on his side and faced me, stroking my cheek with his rough fingers.

"I don't know. There's work, and Sammy." I pulled my face away just enough to break from his touch.

"Natalie, I love you. I still love you, a million years later. But I can feel you pulling away from me lately."

The same anxious tension I'd felt at the sound of Charlie's name began to build in me again. "Pulling away? I'm not pulling away. I'm just busy. That's nothing new. I've been busy since med school. I'm sorry if I seem distant. I'm a distant person, Peter. You know that. You've always known that. You knew that when you married me and—"

He put two fingers to my lips. "I don't care why. I just want to fix it." Peter moved his body awkwardly toward mine, running his hand down my bare arm and resting it on my hip.

His touch felt dirty and unwelcome, and I hated that fact. I hated the panicky, nauseating feeling that was so difficult to fight. I hated that this was my husband yet I didn't want to touch anyone except Charlie.

After I allowed Peter to make love to me for fifteen minutes, he was asleep, and I was putting on my fleece robe and making my way to my office. It was some time after midnight, but I knew rest wouldn't help me. There was no rest inside of me.

It had been more than a week since I'd seen Charlie, and every morning I awoke expecting the longing to go away. But it never did. Instead, I hurt in ways that caused my skin to itch with a restlessness I couldn't escape.

The pain was excruciating at times, leaving me momentarily near tears if I couldn't be close to her, and then, just as quickly, I was elated. For a person who'd made sewing up bullet holes and treating gastrointestinal upsets a life's calling, I'd never considered myself crazy before. But the emotional whirlwind I found myself in nearly every second of every day was unnerving and, I imagined, as close to insane as I'd come. Some terrible love song seemed to be stuck on repeat in my brain, and I couldn't shut it off.

I had based everything in my life so far on logic and rational understanding. Even my decision to marry Peter had been more about a well-meaning partnership than about feelings. Now everything in me felt out of control—as if my emotions were now dictating my thoughts, and feelings were overwhelming all sense of reason. And yet, that same eager restlessness that built in me until I didn't think I could go another minute without her was the most raw, beautiful rush I'd ever known.

It was several minutes before I realized I was sitting at my computer, inspecting Charlie's electronic medical records for her phone number.

What am I doing?

Apprehensively, I dialed the number, hanging up just before the call connected. It was after midnight and Charlie was recovering from surgery. Besides, what would I even have to say to her? Calling her was inappropriate on so many levels. Yet somehow, all I wanted was to hear her voice.

❖

On Saturday night, I agreed to let Peter take me to dinner at the only Italian restaurant in Northwood. It was a small, simple place that housed a lot of the local twenty- and thirty-somethings looking for a drink and some cheap food. It wasn't so much that Peter didn't try. When he was out of work, he cleaned the house, took care of our daughter, cooked—just about everything. He just wasn't much of a romantic.

I was fine with this though. In fact, I think it was one of the few things that had drawn me to him in the beginning. He was predictable and easy. Besides, I was never the type to crave weekend getaways or Prince Charming on a white horse. All I ever really needed was stability—someone to stand back and allow me to follow my career. And, in the case of Peter, someone to love Sammy.

To say I didn't love him would have been both unfair and oversimplified. He was a wonderful friend, a confidant, and someone I was willing to share almost all parts of my life with. Besides, that's how it worked—go to college, get married, build a career, have children. There was an order to this kind of thing. Expectations. Why did it really matter if my relationship lacked that sort of fairy-tale-quality romance? I didn't have time for that anyway. Peter was practical, safe, convenient. He was a good man. And, by the time I began to feel things for Charlie I couldn't begin to explain, he was the father of my little girl.

"This is nice." Peter reached across the table to grab my hand.

"Panzinelli's?"

"No. This whole 'going out' thing. I'm glad we're doing it." He smiled tenderly at me and squeezed my hand.

Fifteen minutes into our dinner, before our breadbasket had even arrived, with Peter in his pristinely pressed button-down shirt, I realized we'd run out of things to say to each other. I've heard that two people can never truly reach that point—that there's always something to say. But not with Peter and me. For years our conversations had revolved solely around our daughter, with even our individual jobs becoming dull to each other. And, as it had become painfully apparent, fifteen minutes was about all the talking we had left in us. So we sat there in silence, as I buttered my bread over and over again, and Peter stirred the ice cubes in his Coke.

At a table somewhere behind me, a group of young people was laughing heartily.

"Hey, don't those kids work in the ER with you?" Peter asked.

My heart taking off like a firecracker, I turned slowly to look. "Them? Um, no, I don't think so…" I whispered, turning back quickly.

"It is. I recognize that one from the party. The one who took care of Sam. Charlie, right? Yeah! And there's that nurse with her!"

I turned again, more out of instinct and envy than anything else. My eyes confirmed what I was sure I'd seen seconds earlier; at the large table behind us sat Charlie, with several of the day-shift nurses, and Michelle, sitting so close she was essentially in her lap.

"Hmm, I wonder where our dinners are. It's been forever." I was still speaking in hushed tones, unsure how I could continue to hide from Charlie. Or if I even wanted to.

"Nat, I'm telling you, that's her. And that's the nurse with her, the one with the…never mind…"

"Nice, Peter. Nice. You know she's, like, twenty-two years old, right?"

"Ha! So I was right! It is them!"

"I guess it is."

The boastful, giddy chatter at the nearby table escalated, until it was all I could focus on.

Moments later, our waiter approached. "Here's your chicken, Dr. Jenner." He spoke loudly enough, apparently, for the voices nearby to suddenly hush. An issue with small towns is that everyone knows everyone.

"Natalie! Hi!" Callie, one of the other young nurses with fiery red hair and a sweet smile, called to me. "Hi!"

I smiled politely and offered a small wave, but my eyes were locked only on Charlie. Charlie's eyes, however, were busy roaming the somewhat exposed body of Michelle as she ran a finger seductively down her arm.

"I'll be right back, Peter." I stood up and gently pushed my chair in, making my way over to the other table.

"You look like a new woman," I mumbled sarcastically, as I slid up next to Charlie.

She looked up from her staring contest with Michelle's breasts. "Hey, Natalie. Good to see you."

"You seem to be doing well, considering you had surgery ten days ago…"

"But who's counting, right?" Michelle reached out and placed Charlie's face in her hands, turning her back toward her.

"Why don't you and Peter join us," Jen, who'd been a nurse at Northwood since I was a new attending, said sweetly.

"Yeah, Nat…Why don't you and Peter join us?" Charlie snapped.

"Charlie? Can I speak with you?"

Michelle looked up at me with a snarl on her imposing lips.

"Go ahead," Charlie responded.

"Alone?"

Michelle's snarl intensified until I thought she'd begin to growl.

Charlie leaned close and whispered something into Michelle's ear, which provoked a giggle reserved for the bedroom, and got up. She followed me into the hallway leading to the restaurant's kitchen. "What's wrong?" Charlie asked.

"What's wrong? You really don't know?"

"No?"

"First of all, you're ten days post op! And you're out here drinking and…and…doing God knows what with Michelle, and you're putting yourself at risk for—"

"Eleven days, actually. And I'm fine. My incisions are healing, my pain's gone, and I'm all done with my antibiotics. I'm fine."

"You are not fine! Your appendix almost ruptured, and here you are acting like—"

"Christ! Natalie, do you ever stop being a doctor and just live?"

Her tone knocked me over, leaving me bracing myself against the wall with one arm. "Oh, you mean like you're 'just living' out there with Michelle?"

"Who I sleep with really has nothing to do with you. You're married!"

"You're right. It has nothing to do with me. And I don't give a shit who you take to bed."

She inched closer to me with an odd cocktail of confrontation and desire. "You sure? Because it sure as hell seems like you give a shit." Charlie pulled me against her with her magnificent hands and closed the breath of space between our lips.

A voice inside me so quiet it was nearly silent told me to stop this—told me this was wrong. But the overwhelming need that engulfed me devoured the small voice, and Charlie's warm mouth met mine. Her hands roamed my body, running a finger inside my front pockets and tracing the button on my jeans. She gripped my hips hard and guided me through a nearby doorway.

"The bathroom? Really?" I teased her, in between rounds of tugging at her earlobe with my teeth.

"Does it really matter, at this point?" she said proudly, sensing just how much I needed her.

I answered her with a hard, passionate kiss. I'd lost track of all time and purpose as I fumbled naively with the buttons on Charlie's shirt, moving my hands carefully up her hard stomach. Her breath came in short gasps, and I'd never been so turned on by how much someone wanted me.

"Are you sure about this?" Charlie asked, pulling away from my touch just slightly.

"I'm not sure about much anymore," I admitted. "But this," I traced the outline of her lips with my fingertip, "right now," her tongue brushed my skin, shooting shivers through my body, "I'm sure about." I moved toward her and kissed the hollow space between her collarbones, sinking into the warmth of her hands as they rubbed the insides of my thighs and carefully grazed my breasts, as if she were afraid the moment might shatter into a million pieces like a dream. I gasped as she slid underneath my bra and softly brushed my skin. Heat burned uncontrollably in every part of me, and I wanted to feel Charlie everywhere.

A knock at the bathroom door caused us to slow down for a moment. A second knock caused us to stop. There was no third knock. In walked Jen, her face the picture of shock and disgust. "Oh, my God…"

"Jen…" I said, without anything else to continue with.

"Oh, my God." She stared, appalled, taking in the image in front of her: me, back against a tattered, off-white sink, blouse pulled up almost over my head. Charlie, standing between my open legs, shirt unbuttoned and falling off, hair in messy pieces. This was certainly something to be shaken up by.

"Jen, I…"

Neither Charlie nor I moved from our undeniably compromising positions in Panzinelli's cramped, outdated bathroom. I was frozen, stuck to twenty-six-year-old Charlie like I'd never leave, as Jen continued gawking with the same mortified eyes.

"I'm so…sorry?" Jen stammered, fumbling with the doorknob.

"Hold it." Charlie's commanding tone stopped her mid-step, as I looked down at her from my perch on the sink. "We could stand here and say 'this isn't what it looks like,' or something clichéd like that…"

"But?"

"But this is exactly what it looks like." Without thought, I ducked my head in a sudden burst of shame. The small diamond band on my left hand caught the overhead fluorescent light, and a pang of guilt shot through me like a dart. I was momentarily sickened with myself, with my life. But all other feelings that fought their way to the surface that night seemed trumped by one of pure, juvenile elation. I was caught, red-handed, making out in a bathroom. At thirty-nine years old, I was finally acting like a teenager. And I wasn't sure how to take any of it.

"So Jen, here's the deal," Charlie said, gracefully pulling her steady body away from its place between my shaking thighs and buttoning her blue oxford shirt. "This didn't happen, okay? Please. I don't need to tell you the repercussions if this got out…

Not to Michelle, or Judy, or anyone. Natalie would lose her job, and let's face it, Northwood can't lose Natalie. You're a good friend to both of us. And you and Nat go way back, right? So please, don't say a word."

Jen contemplated Charlie's plea for amnesty.

"Natalie. This just isn't right. I mean, Peter! And Sammy... and Charlie's so much younger than you! You're—"

"I get it. It's wrong. I know that. And I'm not asking you to keep some big, adulterous secret for me. Just pretend you never walked in here, Please, Jen. As my friend."

She hesitated, glancing nervously at the bathroom door. "Okay. Okay, I never walked in here. But next time, lock the damn door?"

Charlie and I breathed unison sighs of sweet relief as she allowed herself to inch back toward me and rest her hand on the outside of my leg.

"But I still think this is wrong, on so many levels, Natalie. In fact, it's wrong on just about every level I can think of..." As Jen continued to preach, I watched Charlie's eyes examine the small gold crucifix hanging on Jen's neck for what I'm sure was the first time. "And for Pete's sake, pull yourselves together. You look like a couple of horny kids."

Red-faced and huffing, Jen turned and left, and Charlie and I were alone again.

"Holy hell," she said, as the fear she'd been hiding finally poked through her evasive surface.

"I know." I allowed myself to be still for just a moment, reveling in the feeling of my still-bounding pulse pushing up against the walls of my body. A thin coat of icy sweat had built up on my brow, and my ears burned like hot ash. *Don't you ever stop being a doctor and just live?*

"So, do you think she'll keep our secret?"

"Charlie." I pleaded delicately, brushing the short bangs from her glistening forehead. "There is no secret...we can't."

"Oh, Christ, really? This bullshit again?" Her tone changed so quickly I recoiled from her touch. "I don't get you straight women. One minute you're humping my leg in a bathroom and the next you're telling me to fuck off."

I paused to consider my next move, noting the hurt in her voice that melted her anger away. "Look, I don't know what I'm doing here—"

"You could have fooled me." She scoffed.

"I'm serious." I brushed her cheek with the back of my hand. "This isn't some kind of sorority-girl experimentation. It's just happening. And I have no idea what it means or what to do about it." I pulled my fingers through my hair, tugging at it until the pressure faded into the confusion and desire that was so intense it ached. This was not my life. This was some kind of made-for-TV movie or, maybe, the thrilling, unpredictable existence of someone else. But surely I wasn't myself.

"So then…do I see you again?" Charlie flickered impossibly long eyelashes in my direction and smiled shyly.

"Clean yourself up, Charlie," I mumbled, grabbing her shirt lapels hard and kissing the divot on her forehead.

We plotted our exit so no one would notice. But the glares Jen directed our way were like road flares, and everyone at the table seemed to suspect something. Or maybe I'd just added paranoia to my growing list of faults.

"Where've you been?" Michelle pouted, throwing one arm behind the chair.

Charlie sat down in, her breasts so close they were nearly in her face. "I ordered us some more drinks."

I stood in front of them just long enough to watch Michelle trace her fingers under Charlie's collar before turning to return to Peter.

"Sorry, work friends. Jen can talk the ears off a worm."

"It's okay. I mean, you don't see them every day or anything," Peter responded. He hated sharing me with other people, his jealousy sometimes coming up as uncharacteristic anger.

"Peter, you're being childish. I couldn't just up and leave. That would have been rude."

He paused a minute, pushing the feelings back down. "So where'd you and the medic kid run off to?" he asked, with relatively little suspicion in his tone.

Heat exploded into my cheeks and panic engulfed me. "To the bathroom. She's…uh…applying to medical school and needs some advice. You know, recommendations and what not."

"Oh, well, that's nice of you." His furrowed, thick eyebrows lightened with a smile. "She seems like a nice girl. Really bright. Kind of reminds me of you at that age, actually."

"Don't say that. Please, don't wish that on her."

❖

Peter and I returned home to find Sammy sound asleep, wrapped in her pink Disney blanket and drooling quietly.

"She's been doing really well lately," Peter whispered, reaching out and putting a soft arm around me.

"She really has been. Look at how well she's been doing with strangers." I halfheartedly pressed my cheek against his chest and placed a hand on his stomach.

"I remember when she'd cry and cry whenever you left the room."

"Those days are definitely gone. In that sense, I guess she's pretty typical."

"I keep thinking about how good she was the last time we had to take her to the hospital—with Charlie and the others."

A cold chill wracked my bare arms, and I resisted the undeniable urge to pull away from him. "Come on," I said hoarsely, kissing Peter at the base of his neck, "let's go to bed."

Peter grabbed both my hands and pulled me into our bedroom. "You don't have to tell me twice."

With all the passion I could manage, I reached up to him, the father of my child, and placed my hands on his chest, kissing him with so much force he had to prop himself up on the bed. If I kissed him hard enough, wished hard enough, maybe I wouldn't keep thinking about Charlie.

Peter wrapped his arms around my waist and pulled me toward him, until we were so tangled in sheets and blankets I could hardly see my way out. His fingers eagerly combed my buttons, fumbling like an adolescent boy in the backseat of a car. With every stroke of his rough, clumsy fingers, I breathed him in and Charlie out, until I was able to disappear under a cloak of comfort and desire. Peter was my best friend. He was Sammy's father. And in that moment, if only for that, I loved him more than I had words for.

CHAPTER SEVEN

Charlie slipped into the chaos of the day so smoothly I almost didn't notice her. In fact, I wouldn't have, if it hadn't been for the faint trail of sweet musk that was so distinctly her, it made every muscle in my body tighten. I was instantly on fire. I didn't even need to turn around to know she was standing behind me.

"Good morning, Dr. Jenner," she said quietly, briefly placing a gentle hand on my shoulder.

"Good morning," I croaked back, looking around in embarrassment. No one was paying any attention to us.

"Relax," she whispered, leaning so close to my ear I could feel her hot breath on my skin, "no one cares." She was pushing every button I had, and she knew it.

A clichéd throat-clear rocked me out of my lustful trance. "Natalie, I have an iffy EKG I need you to peek at." Michelle's entrance, as loud as it usually was, was stifled by the energy pounding between Charlie and me.

"Michelle, good morning. I didn't see you there."

"I'm sure you didn't."

"I'm sorry?"

"I mean, good morning." Michelle smiled obnoxiously.

"This looks fine," I shot back quickly, pushing the piece of paper toward her. Michelle walked away, defeated scowl in check.

"See! Michelle knows something."

"So what? It's just Michelle. Her word's about as good as a convicted felon's around here."

"Well, maybe if you'd stop letting her grope you in the hallways, or at Panzinelli's…or at all actually…"

A satisfied grin consumed Charlie's brilliant face. "I do believe you're jealous, Dr. Jenner."

"Oh, please. I have nothing to be jealous of. And besides, I think it's you who's been pursuing me."

"Oh, you do? That's funny. Because I distinctly remember you being the one who pulled me into the on-call room and mauled me."

"I did not maul you. I don't 'maul.' Now go away. I have patients to take care of." I playfully pushed her chair away from mine.

"I will if you'll have dinner with me."

Panic gripped at my gut, climbing its way up to my throat with a sickening wave of twists and turns. I'd told Charlie this was more than just some sort of juvenile experimentation to me. But I still wasn't sure what it was. A date? I was married. I had a husband and a daughter. I had a life. Christ, I was straight.

"Charlie, I—"

Judy entered my small cubicle briskly. "Natalie, we have an MVA about five minutes out. Unrestrained driver and passenger. Not sure about injuries, but it sounds like it could be legit. We could use you in there too, Charlie." She walked away with purpose, muttering something to herself I couldn't quite make out, although I was fairly certain the words "joined at the hip" came up.

"You got lucky this time, Doc," Charlie teased me, moving toward the trauma room, "but I'm not one to give up that easily."

"No…no, you certainly aren't."

A few moments later, two paramedics wheeled in a young

man, strapped to a gurney in several places, screaming drunken obscenities.

"This is Tom," one of the medics said calmly.

"Hey, fuck you, man!"

"Tom was the unrestrained driver of a car that took a little nosedive into a tree off the highway. He's complaining of belly pain, but mostly it's his left femur that's bothering him."

"My leg fucking hurts, you douche bag!" Tom shouted again.

"Yes. His leg hurts. We gave him a little fentanyl in the field, but his pressure's pretty soft at this point so we didn't want to push it. Oh, and Tom here admitted to us that he's been drinking."

"I told you! I had two beers!"

"Were they served in fish bowls, Tom?" Charlie interjected, stepping up to the head of the bed with her familiar swagger that did things to my knees I'd only ever been told about.

"Listen, you fucking dyke!"

"Whoa, buddy." John, one of our security guards, moved his six-four frame until it hovered over Tom's restrained body. "You don't talk like that in here, got it? This is my hospital, and I won't tolerate it."

"Fucking faggot," he growled, as I watched his face contort. By the time either John or I realized what Tom was doing, Charlie had slapped an oxygen mask over his mouth and watched as the wad of saliva he'd been aiming at us reflected and trickled back down onto his lips. Everyone in the room chuckled to themselves.

"You don't need to call me names, Tom," Charlie said, coolly pushing the mask tighter onto his face with a sort of Steve McQueen finesse. "And besides, John here? He's married with two beautiful girls. You can at least get your facts straight."

The laughter in the room increased to audible levels as John approached Charlie and clapped her on the shoulder. "Thanks, kid."

"That's what you get for trying to stick up for Charlie," I whispered to him.

"Tom, I'm Dr. Jenner. What happened today?"

For the time being, the inebriated man managed to answer all of my questions without name-calling and only limited cussing. And, after feeling relatively confident his only injury was a fractured leg, which wasn't going to kill him in the upcoming hour or so, I left the room.

❖

"Hey, bitch!" At first, I was able to ignore the shouting coming from Tom's direction. After all, agitated patients are a day-to-day routine in an emergency room, and you become pretty gifted at tuning them out.

"Hey, bitch! I need more pain meds! My leg fucking hurts!" Nurses passed by Tom's room without making eye contact. No one wanted to deal with him.

"Bitch! Yeah, you!" he yelled, catching me looking up from my charting. "I want my fucking pain meds! Now! Let's go! What are you, fucking deaf?"

In an instant, Charlie was there, standing at my side. "Want me to take care of him?" she asked, a thick coat of concern painted in her voice.

"Charlie, please. I'm perfectly capable of fighting my own battles. I've been dealing with idiots like him since before you were even—"

"I know, since before I was even born. You're old, I'm young, blah blah blah."

"Yes. And besides, you don't have to get all alpha male with me here."

"Stay with me, Nat. The things that work on most women, they don't work on you."

"Now you're getting it." I stood up, patted her gently on

the back, and walked sternly into Tom's doorway, although she remained tightly in tow.

"There you are, you bitch! Can't you see I'm in fucking pain here? What the fuck is the matter with you?"

"You're not getting anymore pain medicine, Tom. You're drunk. You're disrupting the entire hospital. And quite frankly, you're a pain in the ass." Tom suddenly fell silent. "Oh, and that's Dr. Bitch to you."

❖

It was sometime in the early afternoon before Charlie made her way over to my desk again. "You can't talk like that," she said abruptly, kneeling down next to my chair and looking as far into my eyes as she could.

"You're right. I was pretty harsh, I know. If management gets a complaint from that piece of—"

"No. I'm not talking about management." Her soft, puffy lips curled up into a seductive smirk. "I'm talking about me."

"Oh, like anybody could ever offend you."

"You didn't offend me. But when you get tough like that… it turns me on like you couldn't even imagine…" She ran her fingers softly down the open collar of her shirt, tracing the strong muscles of her chest and neck until my heart was bounding in my temples. "Seriously. I'm trying to work here." She smiled again and walked off to restock one of the lab carts.

"Judy? I'm going to take a quick coffee break," I said, just a little too loudly, making sure Charlie was well within earshot. "If you need anything, just have them page me and I'll be right there." Charlie turned from her cart and flashed me such a subtle grin I had to question if I'd even seen it at all.

❖

Five minutes after arriving on the roof of the hospital, the door cracked open and Charlie swung through, approaching me slowly, as if to let me take in every piece of her I could.

"Coffee break, huh?" she said in a husky voice that ached with everything I knew she wanted from me. Everything I wanted from her.

"Oh, right...the coffee is...well...it was old so I..."

"Uh-huh," Charlie said, moving so slowly toward me now I had to resist the need to reach out and pull her into me.

I'd run out of words. And besides, words seemed irrelevant when she was standing so close to me. I couldn't do anything but place my hands on her broad shoulders and melt into her lips. They were the softest, most incredible lips God had ever invented, no doubt. And when I kissed them, when I got hopelessly lost in them, I didn't have to think about passion. I didn't have to analyze what I was feeling in order to make it grow exponentially. I didn't have to dig for reasons why they felt so damn good. In fact, thinking had very little to do with it. Kissing Charlie was like slipping into warm water. The perfection that accompanied it quickly dissipated into nothing, until all I had left to do was revel.

"God, I've been waiting all freakin' day for you to do that." She groaned, pulling at the waist of my scrub pants, then leaned down and gently teased my bottom lip with her teeth until my breath came in ragged fits.

"How do you do that?" I gasped.

"Do what?" She ran her tongue softly around my mouth, sending waves of pleasure all through my body.

"Kiss like that."

"Just because I'm half your age doesn't mean I don't know a thing or two." She was teasing me, her hand at my waist beginning to untie the drawstring to my scrubs.

"You are not half my age," I snapped, pulling her forward until my back was up against the door. She slid a thigh between my legs and pushed herself harder into me. "And you don't know anything yet," I whispered, grasping her hips and spinning her around. I kissed her everywhere, starting with her damningly tempting lips and trailing down her neck, the small hollow space between her collarbones, down her chest, until the collar of her polo stopped me from going any farther.

"Take your shirt off," I heard myself insist.

And I watched as Charlie pulled the bottom of her shirt out and over her head, in a motion so painfully slow it took all the willpower I'd learned in medical school not to actually rip it off myself. It was the first time I'd seen her so exposed, aside from our encounter during her surgery. I gawked at her unbelievable figure, with shoulders even better and muscles even more perfectly defined than I'd remembered.

Her Irish skin had begun to take on color in the spring months and looked as smooth and firm as I'd imagined. Her stomach was tight and flat, and I could still see the healing incisions from her recent ordeal. Late-afternoon sunlight framed her face, highlighting her chestnut hair with hints of heart-stopping gold, until I was almost positive she was nothing more than an image from a very pleasurable dream.

"You are…absolutely breathtaking…" I moved to her again, allowing my hands to explore her hard curves and smooth skin. Charlie felt better than anything I'd ever been near in my thirty-nine years.

Without warning, she grabbed my shoulders, kissing my face and sucking gently on my neck until my legs felt ready to buckle. Her fingers reached eagerly for my top, moving up the inside of it to lightly touch me before finally pulling it over my head. There would be no going back, as Charlie reached to undo my bra, trailing her lips down my stomach. My head spun uncontrollably, and I used every ounce of strength I had to keep from falling over. I was enamored by her every touch, her every breath I felt escape against my skin. The heat in my face was suffocating, but I felt freer than I ever had. Her fingers were the incredible blend of delicate deliberation and mindless ravaging, as they traced circles around my entire body until I lost all strength to even consider resisting.

"I want you to touch me." I gasped, gripping her wrist and placing her hand against me.

To my chagrin, Charlie stiffened, gently pulling away from my embrace.

"What's wrong?"

"You've never done this before," she said sweetly.

"I know." My gut-ripping embarrassment must have been more apparent that I'd hoped, because Charlie took me back into her arms and cradled me.

"No, no, no…Fuck no. I didn't mean it like that, Nat. I wasn't saying you don't know how to…Or that you were…Oh Christ, no!"

I smiled again, softly pulling her hands from around my shoulders and moving them to the inside of my thighs. "Then touch me."

I watched her as she seemed to physically stop herself from going any further. "I want to…Trust me. I want the hell out of you…I've never…ever…even come close to wanting anyone like this. You make me crazy."

"I doubt it's as crazy as you make me…" I pushed her hand a little farther to the band of my thin scrub pants, tempting her last ounce of will to push me away again.

"Oh, I'd bet on it. You're beautiful, and sexy. Not to mention brilliant. You walk into a room and everyone stops to watch. You're strong enough to take control of every imaginable situation, but soft enough to stand up here on the roof with me and attempt to get me naked. Anyone would be lucky to have even one moment of this. I won't bother questioning why I've been privileged enough to have several. Or why you seem to want me right back.

"But I will tell you this—you've never done this before. You're an incredible doctor. You were no doubt a flawless student. And I'm sure, as much as it pains me to think about it, you're fucking incredible in bed. But I don't think I want this to happen on the roof of the hospital, during a bullshit coffee break…where I have little to no control of the situation."

"It's always about control with you, isn't it, Charlie," I said sternly, teasing the line of her jaw with my fingers and kissing the tip of her ear.

"I have to try to keep some…" she managed to say through scattered gasps of air.

"Well, for the record," I pulled away with an agonizing need that hadn't even come close to being met, "you have plenty."

❖

"Where's your coffee?" Judy asked, as I sat back down at my desk.

"My what?"

"Coffee? That's where you went…isn't it?" she said innocently.

"Oh. Coffee. Yes. Of course that's where I went. Cold, it was…Not good, so I…"

Judy examined me closely for a moment. "Right. Well, anyway, you didn't miss anything."

I could feel Charlie grinning from nearby as she pretended to study someone's chart.

CHAPTER EIGHT

I woke up to my alarm clock buzzing at five thirty a.m. And for the first time, I actually needed it. That night, I'd slept better than I could ever remember, with the feeling of Charlie's hands on me penetrating through my dreams and onto my skin. Peter huffed as I reached over to hit the snooze button, and my stomach sank quickly to the floor. For a moment, I was rocked back to a reality I couldn't sit still in any longer, and all I wanted was to turn around and see Charlie's face.

"It's early," Peter muttered.

"I know, but we have to get going to make it to the airport on time."

He leaned over and kissed me on the forehead, a devilish look clouding his dark eyes. "We do have a little time…"

"Peter," I said, pulling quickly away from his gaze, "not now. There's too much to do."

"So are we going back to having sex, what, three times a year now? Was the other day just a fluke?" He practically snarled.

"No. That's not it and you know it. Don't start griping about how much sex you're getting."

Instantaneously, the bedroom door creaked open, and Sammy poked her head in.

"Hi, baby. You're up early. Come here," I said, relieved to temporarily avoid the topic of the hour with Peter. Sammy ran to the bed and snuggled in between us. "Are you ready to go see Grammy and Grampy in Florida?" She smiled and clapped her hands together.

"I'm getting in the shower. You girls be ready to leave by seven!" Having finished his temper tantrum, Peter stood up and walked to the bathroom with a smile.

❖

Somewhere between the baggage check and the first security checkpoint, a tornado of emotions that didn't quite seem to fit overcame me. I was leaving for a week with my family. With Peter's family. With my husband. And Charlie had no idea.

I thought hard as the TSA officer patted my sides and ushered me through. What were the rules for this kind of thing? Were there rules? As much as I hated the word, an affair was exactly what it was.

Everything about my life so far had been built around rules and protocols. That was how my father raised me and how I was raising my daughter. It was everything I knew. But an affair doesn't have any protocols, especially an affair with another woman. Somehow, though, I felt an overwhelming sense of guilt for not saying good-bye to Charlie.

Instinctively, I reached into my bag and took out my cell phone. I had Charlie's number. I could call her anytime. But what would I say? I'm at the airport, about to take off for a vacation with my husband. Sorry I didn't tell you. See you in a couple of weeks.

That felt beyond asinine. With nothing left to do, I put the phone away and caught up with my family.

And as I settled into my seat next to Sammy, a new feeling bowled me over—one I never expected while sitting between two people who loved me to the ends of the earth and back. I was lonely—to the point where I ached from somewhere so deep, it almost felt like hunger.

I should have said something to Charlie. What kind of person was I to not only cheat on my husband, but to then cast her aside like some one-night stand? But beyond that, I missed her. Knowing I wouldn't see her, touch her, even hear her voice for at least the two weeks I'd be gone left me feeling cold and empty, with a sort of sadness so real it terrified me to the core.

❖

"Honey…wake up…we're landing." Peter's soothing voice rocked me out of a sleep I wasn't aware I'd been in.

I'd never been much for sleeping. For as long as I could remember, I'd been happy to function on six, even five hours of rest a night, going into the hospital for at least a twelve-hour day fueled by adrenaline and coffee. But lately, since I'd gotten to know Charlie, so to speak, I'd been sleeping almost constantly—in between patients, on the couch at home on days off, whenever and wherever I could.

"You fell asleep again."

"How long was I out?"

"I'd say since about New York. Are you going to make that doctor's appointment now?" Peter prodded me delicately.

"Peter, I am a doctor. Nothing's wrong with me. I'm just tired."

"At least get some blood work done or something."

"Oh? I wasn't aware you went to med school this week. I'm fine."

The razors in my tone silenced him.

"How's Sammy?"

"She's fine—watching *Finding Nemo* again."

"Good," I said with a smile, and closed my eyes again as the plane continued its descent into Orlando.

Absolutely nothing was wrong with me. I knew that—at least from a medical standpoint. But I couldn't help notice the tremendous sense of escape I felt drifting off to sleep. It was as if my mind had to find a way to do what my body wouldn't let it. I refused to allow myself to delve into exactly what I was escaping—although, lately, it had become increasingly difficult to deny.

It had become more difficult to get away. Vivid dreams had suddenly intruded on my once quiet and empty state of unconsciousness. Dreams of Charlie standing in the doorway of the trauma room, wearing a stunning smile, the room suddenly bright with candles and rose petals. A patient comes in on a gurney, but neither of us notices. Jen, and Michelle, and the others dance around us, but no one seems to see us there. Those were the dreams I awoke from feeling as if I'd spent a cold night next to a warm fire. I think those dreams were the reason I allowed myself to sleep at all.

Then, there were the other dreams, the ones where I found myself in the middle of an empty field and all I could hear was Sammy crying. I didn't really hear a sound, but somehow, I knew she was missing. No matter how hard I searched, I couldn't find her. She was gone. It didn't take a psychiatrist to analyze the meaning behind those images.

Those kinds of dreams always woke me in a panic. I'd immediately run to Sammy's side, just to make sure she was really okay. And when, inevitably, she was, a new kind of panic would douse me, a panic in which I would, momentarily, allow myself to realize I was, in fact, trapped. My marriage, which I couldn't continue to deny, was submerging me in a sea of irrepressible depression and loneliness. My incredible daughter, as morbid as it sounded, had me trapped. Our daughter. Our house, our cars, our joint bank accounts, our everything. After a decade together, nothing was mine anymore. And leaving Peter meant losing everything.

Whether you're nineteen or thirty-two, when you get married, no one tells you that you don't just marry that person. You marry their family. You marry their friends who become your friends. You marry your friends who become their friends too. You marry into everything they are and become. And when you decide to leave…You can't just leave. You can't just sign a piece of paper, pack a bag, and move on. No one tells you just how much you have to give. Or, if it ends, how much you have to give up.

❖

"She's getting so big," Peter's mother gushed as Sammy raced around the edge of their above-ground pool.

"Sam! No running around the pool!" I shouted after her. She immediately stopped and hung her head. "She is getting big. I can't keep up with her anymore."

"And how about you, Nat? How are you and Peter doing?"

"Fine. Oh, we're good. Keeping busy, you know? Sammy keeps us on our toes."

"You look stressed. Are you sure everything's okay?"

"Oh, sure. Just working a lot."

Bonnie nodded solemnly and folded her hands across her lap as Sammy sauntered up to me, guiltily. "Sorry, Mama," she said slowly, with a stutter.

Everyone around the pool fell silent.

"Sweetie…"

"Did she just…?" Bonnie said.

"Sammy!" Peter raced to her side.

"No running, Dad," she said, more confidently this time.

"She's talking! Sammy! Sammy, you're talking!" I knelt down on the ground and took her into my arms, kissing her ears and head and nose as she squirmed.

"Love you, Mama," she said again, a proud smile peeking onto her face.

"I love you too, baby." My little girl buried her head into my neck as Peter wrapped his arms around both of us.

"This is incredible." Bonnie was shrieking. "I guess a little Orlando air is good for the girl. Maybe you three should think about a…permanent relocation?"

My cheeks gave out against the pull of gravity as images of a life next door to my in-laws with no reprieve from my isolation with Peter aside from a busy Orlando hospital full of empty faces bombarded me. A life without Charlie.

"Mom, you know we can't just up and leave."

"And why not? We have hospitals here too, you know. The university hospital is just down the road. I'm sure Natalie could find work there. And we have a fantastic school system for Sammy that specializes in disabilities. It'd be perfect, and you know it."

"Mom...that's enough. Really."

"Nonsense. You'd consider it, wouldn't you, Natalie?"

"Well, actually, I—"

"Mother. Stop. Natalie is the best attending at Northwood. She's settled there now. The staff loves her." I winced a little at Peter's last remark. "We can't and won't leave."

"I just think it'd be a great opportunity for Sammy. And you wouldn't have to hire a babysitter ever again. Your father and I would be around. It'd be good for everyone. That New England weather has you both looking pale and miserable."

I couldn't argue with the miserable part. "Thank you, Bonnie. We'll think about it, of course," I said politely.

"Well, I say Grampy and I take everyone out for ice cream to celebrate Sammy's big day."

"Ice cream!" Sammy shouted, hugging Bonnie's knees. We all laughed lightly, the tension of the moment melting away with the warm Florida evening.

I was immensely lonely as I sat with Bonnie, Peter, and his father on a nearby bench watching Sammy play. Her chocolate ice cream was dripping from the cone as she chased the geese that flocked around us. The perfect Orlando sunset had begun, and everything around us was washed in orange and red. Peter sat beside me, his arm proudly propped behind my head, as Sammy shouted "bird!" as loudly as she could.

Watching her—being absorbed into her undeniably radiant presence—was the only thing I had left to keep me grounded. Nothing with Peter, or even a long, nostalgic glance at my wedding band was enough anymore to remind me I still had something good in my life. But when I looked at Sammy, it became clear to me all over again; this child was my world. And a man I would love regardless of the impending heartache it caused had brought her into this world.

The sadness that enveloped me like the Southern humidity abruptly reminded me that, given the facts, I wasn't the victim here. I had a lucrative, respectable profession that I looked forward to every day. I had a beautiful, loving daughter who was finally able to speak for the first time in her life. And I had two impossibly good-looking, intelligent, and charming individuals unknowingly vying for my affection.

I was a wife at home with my husband, who worshipped me, and he didn't have a damned clue that, at work, the sexual overtones of everything Charlie did and said fueled me. That this other person, this other woman ignited something in me that had never so much as seen a spark before, and she absolutely, undeniably consumed me—body and soul, mind and spirit, and any other form you could imagine. And maybe a darker, more frightened piece of me wondered if it was even more than that.

Yet I was sad. I was more than sad. Gripping self-pity with roots so engrained in me I couldn't even follow them back had overcome me.

As I watched Sammy run through the grass, spilling the last drops of her ice cream on her shirt, my inherent selfishness finally became evident. I had it all: the perfect vacation, the perfect family, the perfect life. But all I really wanted was to see Charlie again.

❖

"I can't believe she's talking." Peter beamed, crossing his arms over his stomach as he lay next to me in his parents' guest room.

"It's incredible. Now we won't be able to get her to shut up."

"Just like every other little girl."

I laughed and rested my head on his sturdy chest. He was quiet for a long time, staring up at the whirling ceiling fan, and for a panic-fueled moment, I thought he might ask about Charlie.

"It hasn't always been easy for us, you know," he said. I picked my head up slowly, wondering what direction he was taking this in. "I mean, with Sammy, and you being at work all the time. And me having to stay home for so long…"

"Peter, I—"

"No, listen. What I'm saying is, we've had some bumps. But I wouldn't change a thing. Really."

"Yeah?" I smiled politely at him.

"Absolutely. I love you more today than I did ten years ago, when you couldn't get your nose out of those damn med-school books."

Peter pulled me into him, wrapping me up in both arms so hard I couldn't breathe. But somehow, I felt comforted in a way I so badly craved, in the way only your soul mate can really know how. In these moments, however fleeting, I would almost think happiness was actually right in front of me.

Was it so unthinkable to love the way someone loved you? To seek fulfillment in the fact that person would give you the stars and everything in the sky, even if you might not give quite so much in return?

I dozed off to sleep quietly agonizing over the answers, only to have the buzzing of my BlackBerry on the bedside table jostle me awake. Instinctively, I rolled over and silenced it, then let my curiosity get the best of me and see who was contacting me.

I had several new emails in my inbox, most of which involved work, coupons, advertisements, or forwarded messages from friends. But the name Charlie Thompson under the sender list jumped out at me so boldly all the rest seemed beyond irrelevant.

> *Nat,*
>
> > *Where are you? Haven't seen or heard from you in*
> *a while...Longer than I like...*
> > *I miss you,*
> > *Charlie*

I read the message over and over again, stopping to absorb her enigmatic words and simple language that left her all the more desirable. Charlie was masterful at maintaining just enough space to force me to come to her, all the while making me feel like the single most wonderful and necessary woman on earth. I was sure this was a skill she'd had practice with.

Maybe a reply required a little more caution than I was willing to give. But before I knew it, I was watching my fingers type furiously, the glow of the phone casting shadows around the tiny room.

> > *I'm on vacation in Florida. I'm sorry I didn't say*
> *good-bye.*
> > *I've been thinking about you, though.*
> > *—Nat*

I reread my message again, as a new fear was born; Charlie was young. Very young. How many twenty-six-year-old paramedics who looked like that spent much time bothering with emotion? No. Charlie was the type to want something like crazy—until she had it. And I didn't want to become one of those things.

CHAPTER NINE

Three days later, much to my in-laws' chagrin, Peter, Sammy, and I boarded a plane back toward Northwood. And I still hadn't heard back from Charlie. From my window seat, I tried desperately to erase the thoughts that left me cold and hurting. Hurt wasn't something I was altogether familiar with. In fact, people rarely said no to me, mostly because I'd spent my life in the safety of school and medicine. It wasn't even until college that I began dating—if you could call it that.

His name was David Stone, and he took me to the student-union building for tacos a couple of times before I decided I was tired of being the only virgin book nerd in my dorm and slept with him in the tiny single bed at the Sigma Chi frat house. The next morning, I left the building as quickly as I could find my pants and never spoke to David again. That was really the closest thing I'd had to a boyfriend, until Peter. After college, I applied to six medical schools and was accepted to my top two choices. From medical school, I matched at one of my first residency programs and ended up working for the hospital I'd grown up in. Really, disappointment and heartache hadn't been part of my past.

Yet the idea that Charlie was like every other twenty-something-year-old—chasing meaningless dreams and meaningless flings until the next great thing came along—hurt. The pain frustrated me and caused me to lash out at Peter for nothing on his part. This was why I settled for the security of my mediocre marriage. Love always brought doubt and insecurity that just didn't suit my life. Love, or whatever this was I was feeling for Charlie.

By the time the wheels touched down, I fought the nearly uncontrollable urge to jump from the plane and drive as quickly as I could to the Northwood emergency room—if nothing else, then just for the chance she would be there.

❖

"I'm going to run to the hospital for a little bit. I have to collect some charts," I mumbled to Peter as soon as I dropped my suitcase in the living room.

"What? We just got back. And how can you have charts? You haven't worked in a week."

"I'm behind."

"You're never more than a day behind."

"Are you going to interrogate me all night, or can I just go and come back?"

"Fine."

I slammed the door unnecessarily and drove the few miles to the ER in the black night.

What was I going to do if Charlie wasn't there? What would my excuse be for showing up at work at nearly ten p.m. when I was supposed to be just coming back from vacation? Worse yet, what would it look like if I showed up in the middle of the night and Charlie was there? I didn't have the answers by the time I pulled in to the parking lot, but that didn't stop me from walking toward the electric doors, which welcomed me like an old friend.

"Hey, Natalie." Jen greeted me from the reception desk. "You working tonight?"

I mumbled something incoherent, smiled, and continued walking.

Fortunately, no one else seemed to notice my presence in the flurry of a particularly busy evening. No one except Tim, of course.

"What are you doing here, kid?" he asked.

"Just finishing up a few uh…housekeeping things. You know."

He nodded, brushed me off, and went back to the CT scan on the screen in front of him.

As I looked feverishly for Charlie, I thumbed through mail that had been waiting for me. And then, she was there, looming in front of me, her shadow covering the fluorescent lights as she stood above me.

"Welcome back, Doc." She offered me a casual smile.

"Oh, hello, Charlie."

"Glad to have you back."

"Thanks," I replied, discreetly grabbing a nearby Post-it note and scribbling on it.

Roof.

I slid the paper to her, and she unfolded it with a smile. With a swift, giddy grin, she tossed the Post-it in the trash and headed out the door.

Moments later, I followed her, leaving just enough time so no one would place our exits together. I didn't make it beyond the second flight of stairs before I caught up to her. She stood on the top step, hands on her hips, waiting for me with a look I couldn't quite read.

"What are you doing here, anyway, Nat?"

I took a couple more steps toward her and placed both my hands on her chest.

"What do you think?"

"Well," Charlie whispered, circling her arms around my waist, "I know you aren't working."

"I had to see you, okay?" She smiled proudly and traced the

outline of my jaw with her fingertips until my entire body was burning.

"Okay by me."

We kissed for what felt like days, just kissing until I thought I was melting into the walls of the stairwell, becoming part of the fixtures—part of a world where we were the only ones who existed. As Charlie ran her hands through my hair, I thought I might never be able to stop. Just being close enough to her ignited me like I'd never imagined, until I wanted to climb the walls if she didn't touch me.

"Let's go somewhere," I said. "No one will notice you're gone. I promise."

"I can't."

"You're putting the brakes on again, huh?" I joked as I pulled away from her grip.

"No! I mean…yes. I am. But that's not why, this time. I really can't disappear. Mary Van is in charge tonight."

"Right…Sargent Van…enough said." We laughed quietly together as I pulled her in to kiss her one more time.

"I'm glad you're back," she said, shyly, taking my hands. "How was Florida?"

"Oh, you know. Hot. Full of my in-laws—"

"Peter's family?" she asked, an edge of pain in her voice. Sometimes, I think she forgot—I think we both forgot—just how far beyond the two of us this went.

"Yeah. Sammy finally said her first few words, though. It was something else."

"That's amazing! I'm so happy for you…and Peter… Really."

I smiled at her. In moments like these, when I felt her so closely, it was almost impossible to believe there was so much of my life she wasn't a part of. I kissed her slowly.

"Have breakfast with me tomorrow." Charlie groaned through me.

"What?"

"Breakfast. We'll go to Jerry's or something. Nothing fancy. I promise."

"I don't know, Charlie. What if somebody sees us?"

"Nobody goes to Jerry's. The food's terrible. And besides, if they do, they do. You think it'll ever occur to anyone that we're, well, doing this?"

"And what does that mean?"

"It means that you're older than me, drop-dead gorgeous, successful, and just about the most incredible woman I've ever met."

"And you are?"

"Just a dumb kid who doesn't know what she's doing? But got lucky enough to grab your attention."

"I hardly see it that way." I scoffed. "If anything, I think they'd find it hard to believe that a stud like you would want anything to do with an old lady like me." Our laughter was now reverberating through the stairwell, where it would no doubt travel to the halls of the floor. But I didn't care.

"Stud, maybe. But you're hardly an old lady." She kissed me slowly, with more sensuality than I was sure anyone had possessed in history.

"Okay. Breakfast. I work at eight. See you at six thirty sharp."

"Yes, ma'am." Charlie feigned a salute and winked at me seductively.

"Oh, and Charlie. This is not a date." I turned my back to her and briskly walked away, trying to hide the undeniable swing in my step.

❖

The next morning, I was up long before the alarm clock could jar me out of unconsciousness. In fact, I wasn't sure I'd fallen asleep at all. I'd spent most of the night replaying my reunion with Charlie, each time becoming increasingly thrilled and tortured by the feelings it provoked. I was becoming addicted to the spin cycle in my stomach that occurred every time I remembered the way she looked at me right before she kissed me. Over and over again, I would recount her words, reveling in the high they brought. Undoubtedly a sizable part of me loved the way Charlie wanted me. That kind of attention and longing is difficult to detest. Yet so much more was evolving than that.

Trying not to wake Peter, I slipped out from under the covers and to my closet, thumbing through shirt after shirt after skirt after pants. For someone who never put much effort into her appearance, I wanted desperately to trip Charlie up the way she did me on a daily basis. Maybe I wasn't twenty-six anymore, and maybe I couldn't make a polo shirt look quite as good as she could, but it was time I started feeling as good as she made me, all of the time. The effort to wow Charlie enthused me. Everything was new, and exhilarating, and powerful, right down to my choice of blouse.

I left the house at six fifteen a.m., feeling twenty years younger in a pair of fitted dress pants and a low-cut top I hadn't bothered with since Sammy was born. Charlie was sitting at a booth by the window—I spotted her before I even walked in. God, she looked incredible. I stopped and took her in for a minute, inebriated by the way her uncut, untamed hair fell flawlessly over her brow, which furrowed intensely as she studied the menu. Her white, V-neck T-shirt hung effortlessly over her body, clinging to her shoulders and chest. Her eyes were bright, puffy with remnants of sleep, which reminded me of just how enticing it would be to wake up to that face.

Finally, I forced myself to walk into the dingy diner.

"Hi," she said, with a smile that could bring down dynasties.

"Hi there." I sat across from her, picking up the menu that lay in front of me.

"I wasn't sure you were going to show."

"I told you I would."

"I thought you might wuss out or something." She smiled again, this time in a way that reminded me she still had a lot of the world left to see. "But I'm really glad you didn't." Charlie reached under the table and brushed her hand on my knee. For a moment, I thought about resisting, but everything about it felt too good.

"If there's one thing I hope you'd have learned about me by now, Charlie, it's that I don't 'wuss out' of anything. Come on! You've seen me wrestle drug addicts, get elbow-deep in someone's guts, tell off CEOs—"

"Sure, at work you've got a hell of a pair," she said. "But I'm talking socially. That's a whole other realm for you. And to tell you the truth, I think you're a big sissy." She followed with a laugh so charming and infallible I had to laugh back.

"Okay. So maybe you're right. Maybe I'm a little socially… challenged. But I'm learning, you know. We can't all be the confident, effervescent life force that you are."

"If you were half as confident in Natalie as you are in Dr. Jenner, you'd be unstoppable. As if you aren't already."

"How do you always know exactly what to say?"

She pondered my question a bit, running her fingers through her hair and resting her chin on her fist. "It's just the truth."

"How did you get to be so damn articulate though? Everything you say is like…like it was straight from a script or something."

"I read a lot. And besides, I'm not as confident as you think I am…" Her eyes became glassy and I watched her drift away.

"Charlie." I interrupted her musing, bringing her back to the moment at hand. "Let me ask you something."

"Anything."

"What happened to Dartmouth?"

As she opened her mouth to speak, a waitress with leathery skin and tired eyes stood over our table. "What can I get you ladies?" she said gruffly.

Charlie nodded subtly to me, waiting for me to speak. Ever the gentleman.

"I'll have the veggie omelet and a coffee. Please."

"Very good. And you?"

"Pancakes," Charlie said, flashing her a toothy, effortless smile.

The waitress nodded and walked off.

"So you were about to tell me about Dartmouth."

"I don't want to get into it right now. Another time, I promise."

Charlie's hesitation was clear, but I wasn't ready to let the issue go permanently yet. Something kept this phenomenal, bright woman from pursuing a career that she was more than suited to. And I had to find out what it was. But not today.

"Fair enough." I smiled kindly at her.

"So, Dr. Jenner. Since this is our first date—"

"I told you this wasn't a—"

"Since this is our first date," she said again, this time quieter and searching the room to appease me, "tell me something no one would guess about you."

I contemplated for a moment, trying to delve into my own head to find something Charlie might find interesting. "When I was little, I walked in on my mother trying to kill herself."

Charlie's mouth hung open for several seconds, and for the first time since I'd known her, she had no words for me. "Well, that's, uh…"

"Kind of morbid. Sorry." I laughed, and she began to laugh with me. "How about this one? I hate horses."

"Horses? Why horses?"

"They kind of creep me out. And frankly, I find horse people kind of strange. I just find the whole obsession very weird."

"Gee, Nat. I had no idea you were so judgmental."

"Years in an ER will do that you. Besides. Most people wouldn't guess I was so bitter and jaded."

"Yes, they would." She was teasing me.

"You know, I have to be honest with you, Charlie," I said,

after finishing my second cup of coffee. "I thought about not showing up this morning."

"I figured that might be the case."

"I was so nervous. I thought it might be awkward or something. I thought, I don't know, that—"

"That the only thing we have in common is sex?"

"Yes, actually." We laughed in unison again until my cheeks hurt.

"And? What's the verdict?"

"You have yet to disappoint me, Charlie Thompson. Even in the slightest."

Charlie left the cash for the meal, which I found charmingly ironic. Not many people on a paramedic's salary would insist on paying for a physician's breakfast. Then again, there weren't many Charlies out there either.

We left the diner and walked next door to the hospital.

"Well, this would be where we say good-bye and I kiss you good night and ask when I can see you again."

"But?" I said coyly, inching toward her as we hid behind the ambulance bay.

"But it's 7:50 a.m., and we're going into work."

"You can still kiss me, you know." I shuffled closer to her, resembling the hormonal adolescent I was feeling like, and waited.

"Oh, I can, can I?" Charlie grinned confidently, placing the palm of her hand on my face and kissing me, slowly, deliberately, faultlessly.

❖

"Hey, Charlie, did you have Kool-Aid for breakfast again or something?" one of young male medics asked boisterously from across the nurses' station. The workday was already off to a bustling start.

"Pancakes and black coffee. Why?"

"Because you've got red all over your lips. Are you wearing lipstick, Thompson?" He laughed loudly, as I felt my face flush fire from my desk nearby.

"Hey, Sabraski, doesn't your mom wear lipstick like this?" she shot back.

"Funny. You're funny. You were with a girl. And by the looks of that shade of paint, she's smoking hot." Sabraski pounded Charlie on the shoulder as I reached up to cover my mouth with my hand. The obnoxious Jay Sabraski moved on to torment someone else, and I dashed to the nearest bathroom to feverishly wipe down my lips with a paper towel.

Charlie passed me in the hall as I made my way back to my desk.

"Come here!" I grabbed her by the wrist and jerked her into the trauma room.

"What did I do?"

"Didn't you hear that? You had my lipstick on your face!"

"Lots of people wear that color," she said lightly. And it occurred to me that a part of Charlie wanted to get caught.

"Not today. Not here they don't. He noticed. And that moron wouldn't notice balls on a bull. I can only guess who else saw you."

"Nat, relax. It's fine," she said, taking my hand in hers.

"It's not fine." I pushed her away.

"You basically begged me to kiss you out there. It takes two, you know. Don't go getting pissed at me." Charlie turned and walked out of the room.

❖

It was hours before my pride allowed me to approach her again. "Charlie, can I talk to you? Please?"

"I'm busy right now." She grabbed an IV catheter and started to walk away.

"Please. Just give me a second." She stopped, silently daring me to explain myself. "I'm sorry. About earlier. I was a jerk."

"It's okay."

"No, it's not. Really. It's not okay at all. I was scared...of losing my job, of losing Sammy..."

"Scared people might find out you're falling for another woman."

"What? No. Absolutely not that. I'm very liberal. I vote Democrat, for Christ sake! Like I would care if someone thought I was—"

"Gay? See, you can't even say the word."

"Yes, I can."

"Sit down," Charlie told me, calmly, pointing to my chair and taking a seat quietly beside me. "Relax. No one's paying any attention to us."

"Charlie, I—"

"Just listen to me for a minute, okay? My turn to explain. Maybe I don't have two fancy letters after my name yet, or the extra years you have on me, but right now, I have something to teach you. This is what we call the 'straight girl freak-out.'"

"Excuse me?" I mumbled, not liking the way this was sounding.

"Actually, in this case, it's pretty delayed. Usually it happens after the first kiss, sometimes even before. The freak-out happens when it finally occurs to the straight girl that she may be getting emotionally involved with a lesbian. The longer someone's been straight, and the more she has to lose, the bigger the meltdown. And you're about due for one of Mount St. Helens proportions."

"That's ridiculous. I'm not freaking out. You and I are friends. We're friends. That's it."

"Here it is. Freak-out phase one. Denial."

"Holy hell. This thing has phases?"

"Sure. It's sort of like the seven stages of grief. You might call it the seven stages of gayness, really." I had to chuckle a little, although part of me was undeniably uncomfortable.

"Okay, well, let's just say I buy into this straight-girl-freak-out thing you claim I'm doing."

"You are."

"Okay. So let's say I am. What happens now?"

"That's hard to say." The dimples on her chiseled face reminded me just how much she was loving her newfound position of power. "But if you're anything like other straight girls I've made out with, and there have been many…" I reached over from my chair and hit her gently with the back of my hand. "First you'll deny anything's going on between us."

"No fair. I just gave you that one."

"First you'll deny you feel anything for me. You'll say it was just a fluke, or a mistake, or that you were just confused. We've already kind of been wavering back and forth in the first phase for a while now. Next, you'll try really hard to make yourself happy again with a man. In your case, Peter." I winced, trying to hide just how accurate she was so far. "Eventually, you'll realize he just isn't giving you what you get from me, and you'll come back. At least for a while. And how it ends…well, that all depends…"

"Depends on what?" I was completely engrossed in her story.

"That depends on you. You'll do one of two things. In the end, you'll realize I'm better for you than anything else out there, and, penis or no penis, you'll stay."

"Or?"

"Or, you go. The possibility of the big G-word terrifies you so intensely that you give up on happiness, decide you really are just another straight girl, and continue with your easy hetero life."

"Charlie, I'm not gay," I whispered. "That's just not who I am. I have no problem with it. But I'm just not."

"You straight women are so fucked up. How can you put your hands all over me and then say 'that's just not who I am'? Then who are you? Someone who uses people to fill voids left by their husband? Because I don't think that's the Natalie Jenner I know."

"I am not freaking out."

"Yes. You are. Look," she said tenderly. "I'm not here to make any generalizations about your sexuality because this isn't about that. This is about you and me. And that's it. You don't have to label anything. But you feel something for me, and that scares the shit out of you. The sooner you accept that, the sooner you can move on to the next phase of your meltdown."

I paused, suddenly oversaturated with sadness and anxiety. Unable to go on, I picked up the closest chart to me and began to examine it. "I have to get back to work, Charlie."

And without another word, she was gone.

CHAPTER TEN

I spent the better part of a week avoiding Charlie—this girl I so badly wanted, no, needed, to be near again. I was a heroin addict going through withdrawals so severe that I ached, from every pore of my body. Food and sleep held little interest for me, and the only things keeping me from spontaneously bursting into tears, or burning down buildings, were my daughter and my job. I was angry in a way I'd never experienced before. Angrier than I'd ever been at my father for his drinking, angrier than I'd been at my elusive mother for not thinking I was enough for her. Angry in a way that terrified me.

I was attacking everyone who crossed my path. When a patient wanted a refill on his Percocet, I told him he was a lousy user and should get a job. When Tim asked me to stay late, I told him to handle it himself. And when Peter tried to kiss me, or even grab my hand, I told him not to touch me. I was a monster to everyone, save maybe for Sammy.

My friends and colleagues were getting tired of turning a deaf ear to it too. More and more, I'd hear the whispers—"What happened to Natalie? She's so nasty lately. That's just not like her."

And it wasn't like me. The fact that these people loved me probably salvaged my reputation, in spite of my terrible behavior, but no matter how hard I tried, I couldn't bring myself out of the dark, hollow space I'd fallen into.

Charlie was finished chasing me too. Every day I saw her at work, she became more distant and detached, until she was only speaking a few words to me. To watch her life continue as if I'd never mattered—to watch her smile, laugh, exist without me—just fueled the anger that was already blazing, until I was so miserable, I wished I could find a way to exist without myself as well.

❖

"There's a gunshot to the head coming in, Natalie," Michelle said quietly, a glint of excitement in her bedroom eyes. I couldn't help but notice the change in her—as if her sheer hatred and jealousy of me had all but disintegrated and she was almost afraid of me. Maybe Charlie had told her she was done with me. Maybe they were even dating already. Maybe they'd get married and adopt some babies from some foreign country, and she'd become Mrs. Dr. Charlie Thompson.

"Dr. Jenner? Did you hear me?" she said again, with slightly more apprehension.

"Sorry. What?"

"A gunshot…to the head. Fifty-six-year-old male."

"Is he still alive?" I asked, blankly.

"Barely. But yes. They'll be here in about five."

Dazed, I got up from my seat and moved to the trauma room, where a crowd had gathered. Like in an episode of *M*A*S*H*, we stood there, donning gloves, gowns, and masks, waiting for the crew to arrive. I was inappropriately grateful for the distraction of blood and death, realizing that these were some of the only moments left in my life that I wasn't consumed with missing Charlie. I shivered as a gust of shame rocked me. I was a physician, a professional, an adult. This was my job. People's lives were at stake here. The family of this man with a bullet in his skull was trusting me to do whatever it took to bring their father, their brother, their son back. It was time to pull myself together.

"Okay," I said calmly, inhaling a breath of stale, electrified air. "I want respiratory called. Get the intubation kit ready. Let's do this."

Nurses nudged each other, smiling and whispering quietly, and the intensity in the room lit up like a firecracker. Angry, brokenhearted, or just plain fucked up, I had to make this man my only priority. And this was what I lived for.

"They're here," Michelle said, peeking her head out the back door of the trauma room.

The paramedics wheeled in a man, soiled with blood from the neck up, covered only in a sheet stained with red, at a pace that contradicted the urgency of the situation. That's the thing most people don't realize about emergency medicine—everybody takes their time. Because when you don't, people die.

"Twenty-two-caliber gunshot wound to the right temple. Entrance wound. No exit. The family found him in his room right after it happened. No spontaneous respirations on arrival. We could only get a blind airway in him—he's got blood everywhere. He's tachycardic at 121, pressures have been around 50 palp. Pupils are blown. I'm sorry we couldn't do more." The young medic hung his head.

"Hey, I'm sure you did what you could, guys." I gently placed my hand on his back, as the others in the room swiftly moved him off the gurney.

"Someone get me a size 8 tube, please." I moved to the man's head.

Out of the growing group of staff came all five feet three of Charlie, holding a breathing tube and a scope. And for a minute, she was no longer a woman who kept me awake at night with images of her smile. No longer someone who mixed me up so profoundly, I couldn't even begin to function. For a minute, she was nothing more than a brilliant paramedic, and I was immensely comforted.

"Here," she said, handing it to me and holding pressure on the man's neck to help open his airway.

"You want to give it a try, Charlie?" I asked, softly.

"No." She smiled. "This one's all you, Dr. Jenner."

I suctioned the pool of fresh blood collecting in the man's throat and passed the tube easily through his vocal cords.

"Tube's in." Charlie confirmed placement with her stethoscope, and respiratory connected the dying man to the ventilator.

For at least ten minutes, we all stood around, watching the monitors beep and blip, and listening to the ventilators hiss and scream. What was left to do? The rush, the high I'd so badly needed that day, quickly ebbed, and I was left with the same restless need I'd faced so many times before. The man was stuck somewhere between the living and the dead, his heartbeat strong and young and vibrant, his brain destroyed by the fragments of bullet that littered it. What, exactly, were we saving here? There's never time to ask that question until it's already too late to answer it.

I couldn't help but think about my mother. As a child, I came downstairs one cloudy day in late August to find her sprawled in a heap on the floor, an empty bottle of what I could only guess were sleeping pills and a half pint of Patron sitting neatly on my father's desk. There was no note, no warning. I was ten years old—and when my father found us, I was crouched over her, pushing as hard as I could on her chest, just like I'd read in one of my father's books. I couldn't save my mother. I couldn't save this man, Mr. Taylor. And, that day, I wasn't even sure I'd be able to save myself.

For another half hour, Mr. Taylor's heart continued to beat, as his family members came in droves, crying and screaming and hugging, over and over again, until their sadness, their anger became mine as well. Became all of ours. It's so easy to forget, in the midst of tubes and machines and medicine, that these are people, that these "gunshot wounds to the head" are someone's family. We force ourselves to see them as numbers—a blood pressure, a pulse, a respiratory rate, a lab value. We allow ourselves to be cynical and downright cruel, saying things like "Well, he did it to himself, didn't he?" Things that would appall others outside of our world. We say you have to be a little bit crazy to go into medicine, especially emergency medicine. But you also have to be a little bit dead. If you aren't…you'll die completely. And I realized, looking at the man in front of me, who was no more alive than a ream of paper, that we weren't all that different.

"It's time," I whispered to Michelle, who had been assigned as the man's primary nurse. She nodded solemnly and moved to the family's side.

"Mrs. Taylor," I said, "we've done everything we can do for your husband. But unfortunately, he's gone. I'm so sorry." It was a line I'd practiced a hundred times, maybe more, since residency. But it never felt natural. It never got easier. I watched as his wife collapsed into Michelle's waiting arms and sobbed uncontrollably until her scrubs were saturated with tears.

"No! No," she screamed again and again, until her sounds, too, became just another piece of the symphony of death that was playing in the trauma room that day. "I don't understand," she finally said, this time with an eerie calm I wasn't expecting. Everyone in the room looked up from their work.

"Ma'am, your husband…A bullet passed through his brain. He's gone." I reached out and placed a tentative hand on her shoulder.

"But his heart…His heart's still beating, isn't it? The monitor up there…it says his heart's still beating! So he's still alive, right? There's still a chance?" And one by one, the room emptied out, until all that was left were Michelle, Charlie, and myself.

"Well, that's true but…" I stuttered, overcome with this woman's raw, jagged sadness that penetrated the room.

"What Dr. Jenner is trying to explain to you, Mrs. Taylor," Charlie said in a voice as soothing and tender as I'd ever heard, "is that your husband is gone." She moved closer to the woman and put her arm around her shoulder, allowing the woman to place her head on her chest.

"But…his heart…" She protested again.

"These machines here are keeping his heart alive," Charlie said, gesturing behind her. "But that's it, Mrs. Taylor. It's just his heart. It's a series of muscles and electrical impulses moving in his body. But your husband…he's not in there anymore. I'm so sorry, Mrs. Taylor." The woman folded again, grabbing so tight to Charlie's waist that the air was sucked out of her.

"Mrs. Taylor," she said again, slowly pulling the woman from her grip and holding her in front of her. "Do you believe in God?"

She nodded vigorously, wet, round tears leaking from her dark eyes.

"Well, so do I. And I believe that your husband is with God now. I really, truly believe that. So please…be sad. For yourself. For your children and your family. But don't be sad for Mr. Taylor. God's taking care of him."

Tears poured like waterfalls again, but this time, Mrs. Taylor wore a small, almost undetectable smile. "Thank you. Oh, thank you." She hugged Charlie again. "What's your name, dear?"

"Charlie."

"Thank you, Charlie, for reminding me of God's plan." Mrs. Taylor cried some more, resting her head on her dead husband's rising chest. "Good-bye, honey," she whispered softly, taking his cold hand in hers. "I'm sorry you didn't see any other way."

Emotion inched its way up my throat, choking me quietly and finally leaving me in the form of faintly wet eyes.

"Okay. I'm ready now." And Mrs. Taylor took the gold wedding band off her husband's finger and began silently mouthing a prayer.

I nodded to Charlie, who slowly made her way to the

ventilator and turned it off. For what felt like several long hours, the room was silent. No one was passing outside the doors of the trauma room. No one was shouting orders or taking X-rays. And we no longer heard the comforting whisper of the ventilator. There was nothing.

The three of us stood there, watching these two strangers share their last moments together. In one morning—one dark, terrible morning—it was all taken away from them. I watched the monitors above his head as the peaks and valleys of his heart rhythm quickened and then slowed ominously, and I tried desperately not to ask why. I didn't want to wonder what was so horrible that Mr. Taylor would need to leave everything in this world behind. To leave Christmas mornings, and watching his young daughters get married, and grandbabies running around naked in his kitchen, and night after night with his wife, whose world clearly revolved only around him.

The alarming of the machines briefly interrupted the screeching silence. I placed my stethoscope over Mr. Taylor's heart for several seconds, turned off the monitors, and nodded somberly to Michelle. I didn't have to look to know what she was writing in his chart.

Time of death, 9:22 a.m.

I needed a save. I needed someone to walk into my emergency room on the verge of death, and I needed to rip them away from it. I needed to feel useful. I needed to feel needed. Mr. Taylor had asked to die, but his wife had not. And there was no doubt in my mind that a part of her, a very large, nonregenerating part, died that morning too. And it was her death that sent me deeper into my state of unyielding doubt and despair.

"I need a smoke." Charlie's deep voice rocked me from my introverted hell. "Come with me."

Seeing Charlie standing in front of me, calm and confident, steady and strong, sent a bolt of life through me I was afraid I might never see again. And I was comforted in a way that felt like being held.

Without a word, I followed her up to the roof—our roof—where we sat on nearby empty trash cans.

For a while, neither of us spoke. Charlie took a single cigarette out from behind her ear, twirled it in her thumb and index finger a few times, then lit it slowly. I watched her take a drag, exhale plumes of smoke in serene, deliberate patterns.

"Well. That sucked," she finally said, as a puff of gray clouds escaped her mouth.

"Yeah."

"You know, I don't get it." Charlie threw the butt on the ground and stomped it out. "I've lost people before. Remember Gerald? The blown aneurysm?"

"How could I forget?"

"That was so awful. But this…this feels so much worse…"

"I know."

"But why? I mean, Christ, this guy wanted to die! He did it to himself. He got what he wanted, right? So why does it feel so fucking terrible?"

Instinctively, I took Charlie in my arms like a small child and cradled her.

"Because this wasn't fate."

She looked up at me, curiously. "What do you mean?"

"I mean, considering you believe all that God stuff you told Mrs. Taylor in there, then you believe in fate. Right?" She nodded. "And this wasn't fate. This was a man, a young man who still had at least another twenty years left with his family, who ended it all. You know, with the Gerald Greens, you kind of learn to accept over time that you just can't control some things. That God has a bigger plan for some people, and all we can really do is get in the way. They're going to die whether we help them or not. But this guy…Mr. Taylor…he made a choice. This wasn't fate. This was a choice, and we couldn't do a damn thing to stop it."

When she looked up at me again, her face was damp and her eyes were red and swollen. And she clung to me hard.

"But you were amazing in there, Charlie."

She shook her head. "All I did was hand you an 8 tube."

"No. That's not all you did." I placed a finger under her chin and lifted it, forcing her to look at me. "You told that woman that her husband was dead. That's the single hardest thing you'll ever have to do in your life. I guarantee it."

"So what?"

"So, you comforted her, and you showed her that she wasn't alone, at least for a few minutes."

"What does it matter, anyway?" She shrugged.

"It matters. Trust me. It does. You were there for her when she needed somebody the most. When even I couldn't be."

A tiny smile appeared on Charlie's face. "You know," she said, her face lightening, "telling Mrs. Taylor that her husband was dead? That wasn't quite the hardest thing I've ever had to do."

I looked at her inquisitively.

"So what was it?"

"Honestly?"

"Of course."

"The hardest thing I've ever had to do was let you go, Natalie." My heart thumped hard in my chest, and I opened my mouth to speak but realized I had nothing to say. "It's okay. You don't have to say anything. I just wanted to be up front with you."

"I never said I wanted you to let me go."

She looked far off into the horizon, as far away from me as she could manage.

"You didn't have to."

We were quiet again, the unseasonably bright fall sun warming me from the inside out. "Look, Charlie. You are…" I tried to collect the words that couldn't even begin to sum up the complex web of emotions I'd woven around her. "You are amazing. You're strong, and funny, and kind. You're passionate. And let's face it, you can kiss like nobody else."

She finally looked at me, her eyes brightening, and allowed

herself to laugh a little. "Then what happened? Why did you push me away?"

"What choice did I have? This is real life. I can't just leave Peter and run off with you. Yes, you make me feel things. All kinds of things I didn't think were possible. But so what? Feelings aren't enough to build a life on. Feelings aren't practical."

She was quiet again for a moment. "But what's a life without feelings?"

Charlie was right. Was this what my life had been? An experiment in practicality? An emotionless wasteland driven by my own predefined notions of success?

"Hang out with me tonight." The words tumbled out of me before I realized what I'd said.

"Hang out?" she asked, obviously startled.

"Yeah. It's been a terrible day. Let's just hang out. You know, do something stupid. Something that doesn't involve epi or ET tubes or death or gunshot wounds to the head."

"What about Peter?"

"He'll be fine without me. I'll just tell him I'm…I don't know what I'll tell him. Let me worry about that one."

She contemplated my request a while, intrigue written all over her face. "Okay. Let's do it. But I have to be honest with you here, Nat. I'm not a hundred percent on this. I promised myself I wouldn't keep chasing a straight woman. And I really think this might set me back a bit."

"Relax," I said, a hint of desire and empty need escaping from my voice. "You think too much."

I took her face in my hands and kissed her as cautiously, as softly, as the moment called for.

CHAPTER ELEVEN

I wasn't sure what new hole I was digging to bury Charlie, or myself, in as I changed out of my scrubs. And, ultimately, I didn't care. All that mattered that night was the anesthetic effect Charlie had on me. When I was around her, I was numb to everything but her presence and the enormously powerful yearning she left me with. If I was an addict, Charlie was the fix. And that night, I was far too weak to resist, no matter who I had to hurt to get there.

"Where do you want to go?" she asked, leaning against the wall of the lobby in a worn leather jacket and jeans. She was holding a motorcycle helmet and embodying the delinquency and passion I was searching for that evening.

"Anywhere but here."

"I have an idea. But I'm driving." Charlie slapped the motorcycle helmet against my chest and smiled mischievously.

Briefly I considered protesting. I was too old to be riding off on some kid's bike until God knows when. But then I looked at Charlie again, with her oddly feminine machismo and unpolished sense of self, and the numbness took over.

The sun was still out as I slipped on the helmet and climbed on the back of Charlie's bike.

"Hang on tight," she teased me, and pulled the throttle a couple of times.

Without hesitation, I wrapped my arms around her waist, reveling in the feel of worn leather against my hands and a strong back against my chest. "No problem there…" I muttered to myself.

And we took off, out of the Northwood campus and down the main road away from town. Trees zipped by, and orange and red leaves fluttered around us. The air was brisk and stung my eyes with a fantastic pain that only contributed to the growing numbness. It was just me and Charlie, with her weight pressed against mine. I focused only on the way it felt to be close to her again and my undeniable, extraordinary need to kiss her, to lie down with her in some secluded, quiet place where no one could die, or shoot themselves, or ask me for anything.

Charlie steered the bike toward the water and parked it near the inlet. She cut the engine and I climbed off, not wanting to let go of her. With a sort of automated ease, which served to remind me she'd done this before, Charlie stepped off the bike and opened up a storage bag on the side, pulling out a six-pack of beer.

"Do you just keep these with you, in case you get a girl on the back?" I said, pulling off the helmet and resting it on the handlebars.

"I picked them up on my lunch break."

I took Charlie's hand as we walked toward the docks. "Hey, I think the boats are still running. Let's take a ride." I nudged her like a teenager.

"Yeah? Okay." She offered me a cordial smile, but her doubt was still palpable.

It crushed me to see her so unsure about me, about us. I'd destroyed something invaluable between us, much the way Mr. Taylor had destroyed a piece of his wife. And I didn't think there would be any way of getting it back.

Charlie boarded the boat ahead of me, the six-pack stashed in my briefcase, and led me to the bow of the small touring boat. We were two of only a half dozen patrons on the last trip out for the night, so it wasn't hard to be alone. And alone was exactly what I needed to be with her. We hung off the railings, sipping beer out of green glass bottles and watching the sun go down. Her hair flew recklessly in the wind, and the fleeting light framed her features innocently.

"Are you ever going to tell me about Dartmouth?" I blurted out.

Charlie took another swig from her bottle and tossed it casually in the water.

"Well, I guess I can't keep avoiding it. Can I?"

"Not a chance."

"There's not much to tell."

"Try me."

"Okay. A long time ago, I had dreams of going to med school too. When I finished college, I took my MCAT and did pretty well."

"How well?" I asked, forcefully.

"Forty-two…"

"Holy shit, Charlie."

She blushed a little and turned away. "So, I applied to a few schools and got in. But I didn't think I'd ever be able to afford it. My parents were living in a tiny little trailer and working to retire. And I was just a poor medic. I couldn't afford groceries, never mind a $200,000 med-school tuition."

"What happened?" I asked, fascinated.

"Dartmouth offered me a full scholarship."

"A full ride? To Dartmouth? That's incredible! Do you have any idea what it takes to get that kind of endorsement?"

"It wasn't that big of a deal," she said, shyly.

"Yes. It is. But I don't understand. What happened? You should be a resident right now, not working as a medic in grimy little Northwood."

"I like being a medic. And I like Northwood." She turned abruptly away from me.

"I'm sorry. I didn't mean it like that."

"No, it's okay. It's just kind of a sore spot for me still, I guess."

I grabbed her shoulders and turned her toward me. "What happened?"

"I didn't go." She answered curtly.

"But why? You're clearly brilliant! And your bedside manner—that can't be taught. Trust me. You had everything going for you."

"I got scared, okay?" She pulled away again and took a couple of steps toward the other end of the boat.

"You got scared? That's it? That's your big excuse?"

"That's it. I got scared I'd fail, that I wouldn't make it through med school. And if I did, that I wouldn't be a good doctor."

"But I've never seen you scared of anything."

"Well, I was. But now you know. And it's water under the burnt bridge. I'm happy at Northwood."

"It's not too late, you know."

She moved farther away this time, folding her arms against the rails. "Of course it is. Some of my course work has expired. By the time I finish med school I'll be in my mid-thirties."

I laughed. "That's still a baby."

"I'll be almost forty by the time I'm done with residency."

"No, you won't. You can retake your courses here, at the state university, and you'll be done in under a year. That'll make you…twenty-seven? Then four years of med school puts you at thirty-one, and three years of residency makes you thirty-four. That's nothing. People do that kind of thing all the time."

"And where's all that money going to come from? To take my courses again? To take my MCATs again? Besides, it's been ages since I've even cracked a book. There's no way I'd get that kind of score on my entrance exams again."

"You will if I help." I moved cautiously toward her and kissed down her neck, letting my hands explore her body.

"Help? How could you help me? No offense, Nat, but it's been a while since you took a class too."

"Maybe so. But I'll do everything in my power to help you get that 42 back on your MCAT. We'll have study dates and late nights. Whatever it takes."

Charlie smiled timidly. "Study dates? Late nights? This is an intriguing offer. But what about the money? How am I going to pay for that? And what if I don't get another full ride? Schools are getting so much more competitive these days. Kids out there far younger and more impressive than I am aren't even getting in."

"You'll get in. And you'll get the money. There's always a way—loans and government aid. Now stop making excuses and say you'll do it."

I watched her as she stared out into the darkening ocean. The wind blew her hair into a wild pillow on top of her head that I wanted to sink my fingers into every chance I could get. Her leather jacket flapped open, bumping against the curves of her straight hips that I wanted pinned against me. And her eyes held the sadness and intrigue and youth that made her the oldest soul on earth, with still so much to see.

Charlie was the type of person who could say the word and bring the entire world to its knees. When she spoke, people listened. When she laughed, people laughed. And when she tried, she didn't fail. But it was the intangible that drove me to her like a rat to the piper, that made me, against my will, fall utterly and uncontrollably in love with her.

"Okay. I'll do it. I'll give it a shot. One class. And we'll see how it goes." Shattering my trance, she reached out her hand to shake mine, but instead, I squealed like a child and flung myself into her arms. She held me, hard, for a long time, as we moved up and down with the sway of the water's wake. The sun was almost down, and the brisk ocean air was whipping through our clothes.

I pulled away from her, taking her face in my hands. "Charlie, I think I love you."

Her soft, inviting mouth gaped open. "You what?"

Maybe it was the bottles of cheap beer, or the sunset, or the sheer elation I felt thinking about Charlie finally chasing what she wanted. But I was outside of myself.

"You heard me."

"You…think you love me?"

I couldn't believe what was leaving my mouth. In a single moment—a single, clichéd, overdone phrase—I'd opened myself up fully to someone else. The only someone else who had the ability to destroy me.

"I know I love you." And I pulled her toward me and kissed her.

"I love you too. Like you wouldn't believe."

❖

By the time the boat pulled into shore, it was dark. The lights around the small ocean town were bright and warm, and the air was cool enough to send a sharp shiver up my spine.

"You're cold." Charlie pulled off her jacket.

"I'm fine. Really."

"Just take it." She wrapped it around my shoulders and squeezed me tight.

"God, you're like a walking cliché." I slipped out of her grip and took handfuls of her wild hair in my hands.

"Too many Gene Kelly movies." We walked back to her bike, and she hesitantly fumbled with the keys, neither of us wanting to move. "I guess we should get going, huh?"

"Stay with me tonight."

"Stay with you?" She stuttered, innocently.

I wisped my fingers down her cheek, trailing the open neck of her T-shirt. "Yes. Stay with me. What's the matter, Jagger? A little nervous, are we?"

"First of all, I'm not following your outdated pop-culture reference." She was teasing me. "And nervous? Hardly." But she was. I could tell by the slight tremor in her voice and the shaking of her hands as they held my waist. Charlie, who was always so strong, seemed terrified. And it was beyond sexy. "You and I both know that couldn't work."

"You don't have anywhere more important to be, do you? And I know you aren't working in the morning."

"And where do you think we're going to stay? I can't very well go to your place and climb into bed with you and Peter, now can I?"

"I don't know. He'd probably appreciate that." Charlie scoffed at me and contrived a gag. "I'm serious. We'll get a hotel. I'll take you to the Marriott by the water. We'll order room service and get drunk and just, I don't know, get away from it all."

She smiled at me for a long time, obviously contemplating my request. "I don't know, Nat. I don't think so."

"Why not?" I wrapped my arms around her neck and pulled her against me. "Don't make me beg. It doesn't look good on me."

"This isn't you. You would never sneak off for the night, making up some lie to your husband, getting wasted in a fancy hotel with some twenty-six-year-old you work with."

I knew the disappointment in my face betrayed me. "Charlie, look at me." I put a hand to her lips and traced my finger around them until she kissed the tip and gently sucked it into her mouth. Electricity shot through my body at her touch, and I wanted her lips on me. "This is really, really important to me. I want to spoil you. I want to do things for you no one's ever been able to before."

"Oh, don't you worry about that," she said with a devilish grin. "And anyway, you have to learn you can't always get everything you want."

"You deserve the best of everything. And besides," I whispered, bringing my mouth as close to her ear as I could and running my tongue along the edge, "I really, really want to spend the night with you."

"We both know," Charlie said in a raspy voice, and kissed

me agonizingly slowly, "that you're just trying to get me into bed."

"Maybe I am." My stomach churned with a magnificent tension.

❖

"No rooms at the Marriott." I shrugged, tucking my cell phone back in my bag.

"Another time, then."

"No. No way you're getting out of this that easily. I'll keep trying."

Some sort of regatta had clogged up the local hotels, and at eleven p.m., no one could do anything but laugh at me when I called looking for a room.

"Okay, so this isn't going to happen," I said with a long sigh.

"It's okay. Really. Another time."

"Too late. I already told Peter I was working for the night. Don't make me tell the truth now."

"So what are we going to do? I don't think my dingy apartment is really your scene."

I pondered for a minute, wanting to do anything but return home to my stale, painful life. "Let's stay here."

"Here? What do you mean here?"

"I mean let's stay on the beach. Where's your sense of adventure?"

"My sense of adventure? This is crazy!" She laughed to herself.

"Please?" I feigned a pout, grabbing handfuls of her T-shirt and gently rubbing against the front of her jeans.

She smiled her playful smile that sucked the blood out of my head and left me woozy and confused. "You're dangerous, Dr. Jenner."

After a quick run to the closest convenience store for another six-pack, we sat in the sand, knocking back bottles of beer until the black ocean ahead of me bent and turned in a way that was warm and comfortable and anesthetizing.

"You're going to do it, you know," I said.

"Do what?"

"Get into med school. Become a doctor."

She collapsed onto her back next to me and folded her hands behind her head.

"Yeah?"

"Absolutely. I can't wait to see the amazing things you're going to do with your life."

"But there's one thing that still bothers me," she said, propping herself on her side to face me.

"What's that?"

"If I go to med school I'll have to move."

It hadn't occurred to me that Charlie might leave. And in all of my encouraging and pushing her to be great, I suddenly and selfishly wanted to do everything I could to keep her with me. "One day at a time."

She didn't respond but instead continued to squint at the bright, clear stars above her. Every muscle in my body tightened and twisted as I lay down next to her and bent over her, kissing her timidly at first and then with a growing intensity that caused her breath to come in heavy gasps. I knew what I wanted. And for the first time, there we were. No rooftop coffee breaks, no unsuspecting husbands, no death or disease or destruction. No interruptions, except the lapping waves and the half moonlight. No excuses, Charlie.

Her soft hands ran under her jacket that I wore, deftly tracing patterns on my skin. I kissed her neck, and her ears, letting my lips explore every part of her I could get to.

"Nat." She moaned quietly, putting a hand to my mouth.

"No. You aren't stopping me this time. It's perfect. We're alone. And who knows how many other times we're ever going to get to be. We have the whole night and—"

"Shh," she said sweetly. "I was just going to say, take the jacket off." I laughed a little and quickly removed the leather jacket and threw it on the ground next to us. "Now lie back."

I wasn't used to taking orders from anyone, but I slowly and submissively lay down in front of her. Somehow, I didn't mind at all.

Charlie stared at me for so long I began to wonder if I'd done something wrong. "What is it?" I reached up to run a hand through her hair.

"You're beautiful."

I grabbed the collar of her shirt and pulled her down to kiss me, until her weight covered me. One by one, Charlie undid the buttons on my shirt, never taking her burning gaze away from mine. When she reached the bottom, she carefully opened it, like some kind of anticipated gift, kissing my chest and my stomach until my heart revved in every inch of my body. Every place her fingers and lips touched burned.

"You have no idea how badly I want you right now." I groaned, running my hands up her sides and through her hair, finally pulling her T-shirt over her head. My own head swam as her hand moved down my stomach and expertly unhooked the button of my jeans.

"Are you sure?" Charlie asked, kissing my jaw.

"Yes. Dear God, yes. I'm sure."

As she slid my pants down over my knees, I thought about nothing but the feeling of her hands on my thighs—of her skin on my skin, her lips on my lips. The sea wind rushed by, but I was covered in a fine layer of warm sweat. I could picture the epinephrine dumping into my bloodstream, my vessels constricting, my heart pounding from top to bottom, rushing blood to my head. My stomach bowed in a painfully congenial way I'd never felt before. And my breath was hot against Charlie's. Until this moment, I was sure I'd known highs and adrenaline and extremes. But this—this was something else entirely.

The first simple brush of her fingers against me sent a million volts of electricity that caused my legs to convulse and my hands to grab recklessly at her back. The sky around me disappeared as I shut my eyes tight and disappeared under her touch. Her fingers caressed me with expert circles until breathing felt like a chore, and a deep, throaty moan escaped me. "Oh, my God, Charlie..."

She answered by lowering her mouth to my breast and running her tongue along my nipple, taking it into her mouth and gently nipping it with her teeth. Wave after wave of need spread down my body, following the path of her touch. Her fingers moved faster, keeping pace with my breath until I took her in with the air. A fire that had been steadily burning continued to build until it flashed inside of me and ignited my every cell. "Charlie..." I breathed, still gripping her head against my chest. "I love you. I love you so much."

She collapsed against me, where I held her.

We fell asleep to the sound of the ocean whispering to us. Every so often, a car would pass by and its headlights would brighten the dark sky, and I would catch a glimpse of Charlie, sleeping beside me. She was perfect. Peaceful, and stunning, and so able to take on the world. And she was mine. At least for the rest of the night, she was mine.

I couldn't remember the last time Peter and I had really held each other. For years we fell asleep, side by side, in the same bed. But it was nothing like this. Lying next to Charlie was the reason people didn't sleep alone. Nothing else existed outside us, outside of this moment, that could possibly have mattered more.

I placed my hand over hers and stroked her fingers as she gripped it hard. We slept that way, quietly and soundly. And when I finally woke up to the sun peeking up over the water, my hand was still there. At thirty-nine, I'd never imagined something as small, as simple, as holding someone's hand could lead to so much contentment. It was comforting, and intimate, and felt better than anything in the world.

"Hey," Charlie said with a smile as I lifted my heavy head up to look at her.

"Good morning." I kissed her quickly.

"Are you okay?"

"Of course I am." I laughed at her and stroked her arm. "Can't hold my liquor like I used to though. I feel terrible."

"Let's get you home. It's almost seven." Charlie stood slowly and took my hand. We walked wordlessly to her Honda and took the short trek back to the hospital.

"I never thought I'd get to fall asleep next to you," she said, climbing off the bike after me.

"Me either. I wish we could do it more often."

"So do I. Look, Nat, are you, you know, okay, with last night, I mean?"

I took both of her hands in mine and held them to my chest. "Of course I am. It was one of the best nights of my life—second only to when Sammy was born."

"You aren't freaking out?"

"No." I laughed. "I'm not freaking out."

I kissed her good-bye, thanked her, and climbed into my Jeep, feeling empty and alone.

CHAPTER TWELVE

I slept the afternoon away by myself, tossing restlessly and dreaming about the night before. When I woke up, I was tormented with a sort of sick concoction of the sheer elation of just how close I'd gotten to Charlie hours before and the unsettling emptiness I felt without her. I'd never missed someone so acutely, so painfully, after such a pathetically short period of time. It was terrifying.

Somehow, Charlie had not only worked her way into my bed, but also into my thoughts, where she'd laid roots and refused to leave. The intensity of whatever had flourished between the two of us was so unnerving, I trembled whenever I allowed myself to think about it. Never in my years had I even come close to the inexplicable connection I'd found with her.

❖

I spent the next two days in my study, surfing online articles on pharmaceuticals, diagnoses, rare skin disorders—anything that didn't involve Charlie. Of course, everything involved Charlie.

I couldn't read about a two-year-old with a rash without remembering how great she was with Sammy. Or about a stellar diagnosis of some unusual African fever without thinking about the way her face lit up when she'd spot a heart attack from the waiting room. She had consumed even medicine.

Charlie had invaded every corner of my life, like a virulent strain of some disease that brought me to my knees like a weak teenage girl. This wasn't me. And if I continued to let this woman expose me so effortlessly, I would certainly fall apart.

❖

"You're avoiding me again," Charlie said, nonchalantly strolling up beside me as I walked to the on-call room later that week.

"I'm not."

"Yes. You are. You ignored my five text messages yesterday. You're avoiding me."

"I was busy. I didn't have my phone on me."

"All day? Bullshit." But she was more factual than angry.

"Okay. Let's talk." I pulled her into the room behind me, shut the door, and sat on the bed.

"Now?" Charlie said with a smile, and moved forward to kiss me.

"No. I really mean talk."

Her face contorted painfully. "Okay. Talk."

I sucked in the biggest breath I could manage, my heart beating wildly through my scrubs. I had no idea what I was about to do—just that it would undoubtedly change everything. "What are we doing here, Charlie?"

"What do you mean, what are we doing?"

"You and I, this crazy whirlwind thing we have. It has to stop." My efforts felt no different than telling a patient's family their loved one had died—practiced and, somehow, artificial.

"What are you trying to say?"

"I can't keep leading you on like this. It's not fair to you. You should be with someone who can give you what you want."

"You're what I want." She took a tentative step toward me and ran her fingers through my hair with a sort of desperation that broke my already shattering heart.

"Who are we kidding here? I'm married. I'm a mother. For Christ sake, I'm thirty-nine years old. You're just a kid."

She collapsed onto the bed next to me, withdrawing into the wall behind us.

"Come on." I put a patronizing arm around her, all the while silently scolding myself for all the things I'd done, and the things I continued to do, unable to be sure which evil was worse. "This was never going to go anywhere. It was fun while it lasted, but for your own good, it has to stop. Before you get in too deep."

She stood up quickly, towering over me. "Before I get in too deep? Too late for that. I'm in love with you. It doesn't get too much deeper than that! And what about you, huh? This has just been some kind of mid-life crisis to you? Your version of a red convertible and a hairpiece?"

"Okay, I deserve that."

"You know what? You're right. I can do better than this."

My heart screamed a little louder until it thundered in my head. "Yes. You can. I mean really, what did we expect? That I'd just leave my husband, and you and I could run off together?" I forced a laugh.

"Actually, I don't know what I thought. I just thought that you felt the way I did."

"I do!" I whimpered. "I mean, I think I do. Sometimes, I'm not absolutely sure how I feel. And I don't want to take this any further when I don't know."

"After all this—after everything we've been through, you're still not sure." She got up and moved slowly toward the door.

"I'm sorry, Charlie. I'm so sorry—"

"Forget it," she said, turning the handle. "You're right. Consider this my resignation. I'm done trying to win you over. I'm done trying to make you fall in love with me. I'm just done." She opened the door and stepped out.

"Charlie," I called after her. "Friends?"

She hung her head and walked away.

❖

I passed a Barnes & Noble on my way home that night, and something propelled me to stop. Without realizing it, I found myself at the register, a stack full of MCAT prep books and microbiology CliffsNotes in hand.

I'd never been to Charlie's tiny, one-bedroom apartment near the ocean. But she'd pointed it out to me the night we spent on the beach. Charlie was gracious, and kind, and I had little doubt at this point that her feelings for me went beyond some kind of juvenile crush. But I'd crossed a line that day. I'd been so busy trying to uphold the walls around my heart, around my safe little life, that I'd failed to realize she'd also let me in. She'd made herself vulnerable to me. Even through her tough facade, Charlie was not impenetrable to love. She'd loved me. She'd trusted me. And I'd walked away.

"Natalie?" Charlie opened the screen door and stepped out onto the rickety porch.

She was wearing glasses and a worn white T-shirt that did little to hide the outline of her breasts, her hair sticking up just a little from the cowlick in the back that always made her look like she'd just woken up. My heart rattled in my chest like a stone, and my stomach clenched. I'd never wanted anyone so much. No. I'd never needed like that before.

"I didn't know you wore glasses," I mumbled, daftly. It was the first and only thing to enter into my bewildered head.

"Um, yeah. You know, contacts…What are you doing here?"

"Can I come in? It's cold out. And you aren't wearing much." Heat flushed my face as I remembered just how close I'd been to her only days before.

"Oh. Yeah, sure. Come on in."

I followed her, taking in my surroundings. She had very little on the walls, save for her paramedic certificate and a poster of Bullet. "You seriously need a woman around to help you redecorate this place, you know," I teased her, dusting off a statue of a vintage motorcycle with my index finger.

"I don't get many visitors. Or at least not ones who pay much attention to the décor." She smirked subtly, as a vicious stitch of jealousy penetrated my gut.

"Right. So anyway, I was on my way home, and I thought maybe we could start studying. I stopped by the store and picked these up for you." I opened my bag and started to unpack the stack of at least a half dozen books onto her cluttered kitchen table.

"Hold it." Her hand came down firmly around my wrist. "Are we just going to pretend like nothing happened now? From coworkers, to lovers, back to coworkers, or what? Are you my tutor now?"

I eased my hand into hers as she relaxed her hold on me. "Your tutor? I think we could work with that…" I softly caressed her palm with my thumb.

"You're unbelievable." She huffed, pulling sternly away from me and crossing to the other side of the kitchen.

"You're right." I hung my head. "I'm sorry. I don't want to confuse things any more than I already have. But just know this isn't so black and white for me. We ended it because we had to."

"We ended because you had to. Because you were chickenshit."

"Maybe so. I'll try to be your friend. If you can try to be mine…"

She was silent for a moment, running her hand through her hair in the way that made my legs unsteady. "For now, you can be my tutor. We can work on the rest."

That would have to be a start. A start to what, I wasn't quite sure. A start to a friendship? A start to something simple and platonic? Somehow, I doubted that was even possible. But if playing Charlie's tutor meant being in her cramped little apartment, hearing her voice, watching her move through the kitchen as she attempted to hide dirty plates and laundry, knowing she was near, then I'd take it, gladly. "Deal. Let's get started."

"Now? You want to study now?" She stuttered a little and sat on the kitchen counter.

"Unless you're busy."

"Not really. I was just watching the same episode of *Law and Order* I've seen four times already. Want a beer?"

"That'd be great," I said with a smile, and sat down at the table.

Charlie grabbed two bottles of imported beer out of the fridge and popped them open. "So where do we start?" She sat down on the table, facing me, and opened a book.

"Let's start at the beginning. Biology and calculus are the only courses that have expired, right?"

"Yeah, and I don't have to take calculus. Actually, I registered for the late-fall session at the community college, this afternoon."

"You did? Charlie, that's great." I reached up and put my hands on her thighs, but she quickly pulled away. "Sorry."

"Friends, right?"

"Right. Friends."

"So, let's review this biology business. It's been a long time, but maybe it'll come back to me." She thumbed through the book with determination and a disinterest in me that drove me crazy.

"Okay. Let's start small. What's the driving force of a cell?"

"The mitochondria."

"And the transport system?"

"The golgi."

"Well, you already remember more than I do." I laughed.

The next time I looked at the clock on Charlie's microwave, it was ten thirty p.m., and my cell phone was ringing loudly from my bag. "Damn, it's Peter. I completely lost track of time." She nodded subtly, never taking her eyes out of the book she was reading. "Hi, hon. I'm sorry it's so late. I was helping Charlie study for the MCAT. Yeah, she's decided to take it again. I know it's ten thirty. How's Sammy? Good. I'll be home soon, okay? I love you too."

"So? Is he pissed?" she asked.

"No. You know Peter. He's pretty oblivious."

"We're just studying. Tutor. Remember? There's nothing to be oblivious to." And for a moment, I almost sensed a tinge of bitterness in her guarded voice.

"I should get going." I picked up my bag and tossed it casually over my shoulder.

"Thanks for the books. And for all the help."

"Don't mention it. We'll do it again soon, okay?"

She nodded and led me to the front door. "Good night, Natalie. Drive safe."

"Good night." I hugged her tight, reluctant to ever leave her again.

Charlie was the first to pull away slightly, as I moved my mouth slowly but confidently to her face. As she held me tentatively, I kissed her cheek, moving closer to her lips, touching them softly.

"Hey," she whispered coldly, pulling herself from my reach. "Friends. Right?"

"Right. Friends."

❖

I lay awake all night, staying as far to my side of the bed as I could. Every few minutes, I'd check my cell phone, hoping desperately for a message from Charlie. But none ever came. I'd gotten used to her incessant messages—our conversations often lasting until three a.m. I was amazed how they'd quickly become the highlight of any day, when I wasn't able to be with her.

I spent the rest of the night fighting the urge to contact her, until I finally dozed off sometime in the early morning.

CHAPTER THIRTEEN

"I brought Thai," I said, standing at Charlie's front door and holding two paper take-out bags a couple of evenings later.

"How'd you know I didn't have any food in the house?"

"Just a hunch."

She smiled and let me in.

"I made coffee. Strong and black," she said, filling a mug and handing it to me.

"How well do you know me?" I smiled and sat down on the living-room sofa.

Charlie took a seat next to me, keeping a cautious foot of space between us.

"What's on the agenda for today?"

"How about anatomy?" I blushed furiously at my misstep. "I mean, you know, um, the circulatory system."

"Sure. Why not?"

"Where is the electrical impulse of the heart generated?"

"The SA node. Then the AV, then the bundle branches, then...Damn it, Natalie." She suddenly erupted, slamming the book on the dingy coffee table.

"What's wrong?" I was startled.

"I can't do it."

"What are you talking about? You're doing great."

"No. Not the books. This. Pretending we're just friends. I can't do it."

"You seemed pretty all right with it the other day."

"Yeah, well, I'm a good liar." Her head dropped into her hands.

"You had me fooled." I reached out to comfort her. "So what do we do?"

"I don't know. You tell me."

I thought for a minute, running my fingers through the soft, short hair on the back of her head. I needed her. I needed to touch her, to feel her breath on me, her lips. I needed to make her laugh and to be held by her. I needed her youth and her perseverance and her fight. I needed the way she needed me. I needed everything about Charlie. And that need was greater than any sense of right or wrong. This wasn't about losing control. No. I'd already lost all control the moment I met her. "Maybe I freaked out a little bit. Maybe I'm scared. I don't know. Why do we have to label everything? Why can't we just keep things how they were?"

"I never said we couldn't."

"And you're okay with this? This sort of up-in-the-air, day-to-day kind of thing?"

"I don't remember ever asking you to move in with me or get married in Boca. What makes you so sure I'm even asking you to leave Peter?"

I was surprisingly unnerved by Charlie's response. "I'm not sure. I guess I just sort of assumed that you—"

She placed two fingers to my lips. "Don't you know never to assume anything with me?"

I shivered hard as she took me in her arms and kissed me with all the fervor she could manage. She took my hair in her fists, tugging on it gently and biting my bottom lip until I thought I'd combust. I eagerly pulled off her shirt, running my nails up her sides and down her bare back until she was breathing heavily in my ear. "Are you sure about this?" I asked, holding her face in front of mine.

"That's my line."

I pulled her face to me and kissed her with all the passion and need I'd been burying without her. That first afternoon in the on-call room, when I thought I'd never wanted anything so badly in my entire life, seemed like nothing more than a teenage pipe dream compared to the heat that pulsed through me as she traced a path down my stomach with her tongue. She stopped just long enough to tug at my jeans and gently touched the inside of each thigh with her lips until I was burning for more.

My body ached and every muscle tightened as her mouth found me, a loud moan escaping from mine. "Charlie. I need you." I raked her bare back and through her hair with my nails until I felt her trembling from above me. Her breath was hot against my skin, her tongue soft and wet on my body. She gave herself to me until my eyes could no longer focus even through the darkness of closed lids, and my head felt light and airy.

My muscles tightened until I let out one final, deep moan, my body losing all strength. I pulled her up beside me. "You're amazing," I whispered.

She laughed quietly. "So I've heard."

"No. I mean it, you jerk. You're just…like no one else I've ever known."

She silently smiled and nuzzled her head under my chin.

"We really need to get to work," I said, once I was able to find words again. I was lying peacefully against Charlie, her arms wrapped securely around me.

"Huh?" She stroked my hair tenderly.

"You know. MCAT? School? Ring a bell?"

"Oh. Right. Well, I feel like there's a bad anatomy joke in here somewhere, but I'll spare you."

I laughed a little, sat up and slipped on my sweater. "I appreciate that. What time is it anyway?"

"Five fifteen or so. Do you have to get home to Peter?" she asked, sullenly, my heart sinking a little at the mention of his name.

"No. He knows I'm here. I told him I'd be late. Let's get to work then?" I leaned down to kiss her, throwing her tank top at her.

"Nat."

"Yeah?"

"I love you."

I felt my face deceive me. Somehow, I'd managed to pull Charlie in again, my own selfish needs negating any sense of consequence. How many more times could I do this? How many people could I leave in my wake of self-navigation? I was afraid to find out. "I'll put the coffee on." I got all the way to the refrigerator before realizing I was still shaking.

❖

Charlie had started school again, and three times a week she was on campus, studying biology with kids her own age—girls her own age. It would have been dishonest of me to pretend that idea didn't bother me. The truth was, Charlie wasn't mine. Maybe, emotionally speaking, she was. But people like Charlie didn't stay still for very long.

There's a theory in emergency medicine that everyone who goes into it is either running away from something or running toward it. And I often wasn't sure which one Charlie was. On most days, I wasn't even sure which one I was.

Still, there was nothing I could do. We were trapped in this odd purgatory of the not-quite-friends, not-quite-lovers that reminded me very much of Mr. Taylor, in the hours before he died.

A purgatory I'd created.

This purgatory extended from my personal life into my work, where I was forced to see Charlie on a nearly daily basis. Maybe forced wasn't the right word. The nonsensical part of me got out of bed every morning if only for the chance I'd walk through the ED doors and catch her watching me come in. We'd pass each other in the hall, only somewhat unintentionally brushing hands, or hips, or shoulders. And as the electricity cascaded through me, I'd attempt a casual "hello" and try to suppress the elated smile that found its way to my lips.

We would go on with our work, healing the sick and wounded. And in my favorite moments, we were doing it together. I would take a history from the elderly man with a headache while Charlie started his IV and gave him some pain medicine. I'd always loved to watch her work. But every time I did, I seemed to fall more in love with her—and more out of control of my own emotions.

It was late into the evening shift, and the swell of sutures and abdominal pains had dissipated enough to allow me to finish some paperwork over a cup of cafeteria soup at my desk. Charlie was there too, and as I worked, I watched her laugh and joke with a group of nurses by the supply room. The radio was quiet, the patients were quiet, and studying Charlie's smile was making my stomach jump in only the best ways. I was light—as if anything was a possibility.

My heart tripped a little as I saw Michelle approach the group, and although I couldn't make out what they were saying, I hardly needed a script when she tapped Charlie on the chest and motioned for her to follow with a sort of come-hither gesture I could only find lewd and clichéd. A part of me—a part I imagined to be similar to those I'd destroyed in Charlie—died a little as I watched them disappear into the dark, empty trauma room.

I had to follow, even if it meant looking like a lunatic. Walking casually toward their shadows, hoping my legs wouldn't fail me, I picked up the phone on the wall nearby, listening to the hum of the dial tone, praying I didn't look quite as ridiculous as I knew I did.

"You're still coming to Shooters later, right?" I heard Michelle's melodious, feminine voice, maybe just a little bit louder than necessary, carry out the doorway next to me and into my strained ear.

"I think I'll be up for a few games of pool and a beer," Charlie said. That tone…I knew that tone so well. It came infused with sex and lust and desire. It was the one she used when she spoke, right before she kissed me. It was the tone she used when she made love to me on the beach for the first time. Except this time, it wasn't for me.

"Or we could skip the bar altogether and just go right to your place." My skin crawled with envy, and I slammed the phone's receiver back into the wall, interrupting their plans just long enough for Charlie to peek her head out the open door.

"Natalie. I didn't realize you were standing there." She spoke unapologetically.

"Just making a phone call."

"What's wrong with the phone at your desk?" Charlie attempted to suppress an amused grin at Michelle's snipe.

"Broken." I turned and walked off, defeated.

CHAPTER FOURTEEN

H ey! I'm here!" I yelled through Charlie's open screen door. And after waiting long enough without a response, I quietly tiptoed in and placed my things on the kitchen table. The sound of running water propelled me to the closed door of the bathroom.

"Charlie? You in there?" I knocked again, as the water shut off.

A few seconds later, Charlie tentatively stuck her head out, clad only in a sports bra and tight black briefs. My heart jumped into my throat and my stomach turned with need.

"Nat. You're early."

"I know," I said with a grin, reaching out to touch her still-damp hair.

"Actually," she said, awkwardly stepping away from me.

"Dr. Jenner?" Out from behind Charlie emerged the figure of a soaking-wet, statuesque woman wrapped in a towel.

"Michelle?" My mouth hung open foolishly as Charlie moved to my side.

"Michelle was just—"

"Taking a shower with you?" I said, somehow managing to suppress the flood of tears or waves of blinding anger—whichever showed up first.

"Well…yeah…" She placed a hand on Michelle's bare shoulder. "Michelle, do you mind taking off? Nat and I sort of have plans."

"Forget it, Charlie. I thought we had something. But I'm not going to play second-best here. You're a dick."

"Michelle, don't." Charlie whimpered halfheartedly, grabbing her by her elbow.

"Good-bye." In a dramatic huff, Michelle grabbed her clothes and stormed out of the house.

"So, you want to talk about it?" Charlie asked, pulling on a sweatshirt and twisting the cap off a bottle of beer.

"Talk about what? Oh. You mean Michelle, in your shower."

Her face colored. "Yes. That."

"Are you sleeping with her?" I stared at the wall ahead of me.

"Well, we weren't playing gin rummy. And besides, why do you care?" Her tone was harsh and unforgiving.

"Because if she's in the picture, then what the hell am I?"

"I thought we weren't going to label anything." She was mocking me. "Why do you care so much?"

"Because. I do," I said, childishly.

"That's not good enough. Try again."

"Because! Because I want to be the only one you want."

Charlie scoffed and rolled her eyes. "That's selfish as hell. You want to be the only woman in my life, but I'm supposed to be okay with this sort of casual, fly-by-night fling we have going? I mean, Christ, Natalie, I don't have a damned clue what I mean to you. You know that?"

"You really don't know?"

"No! I have no idea. One minute I think you're crazy in love with me, and the next…the next I think you'd be just fine if I walked out of your life right now."

I took her chin in my hand, forcing her to look at me. "I'm not great with my words, or my feelings. Not like you are, okay? Medicine has been my life for, well, pretty much always. But you've completely changed everything. I don't even know which way is up anymore. You mean the world to me."

She was silent for a long time. "Listen," she said, looking over my shoulder. "I have to be honest. Michelle being here was no accident."

"I didn't think she just showed up on your doorstep."

"No. That's not what I mean. I mean, I had her here when I did because I wanted you to catch us."

"But why?" I said, dropping my hand and backing away.

"I thought that maybe, if you saw us, you'd get jealous. And you'd realize what you have with me."

"That's pretty immature and shady, Charlie."

"I know." Her face fell.

"But," I leaned forward and gently nibbled on her ear, "it kind of worked."

"It did?"

"Like a charm." I kissed her neck and chin, trailing my hands up her thighs. "Seeing her here like that," I whispered coyly, "just about made me crazy."

And before I could say anything else, Charlie had me pinned on her sofa, holding me down and kissing me softly until I forgot everything around me.

❖

The house of cards that had become my life was teetering more and more by the moment. I spent my evenings in Charlie's small apartment, laughing, thumbing through science textbooks, kissing her, touching her…Living and breathing her. A sort of freedom accompanied my time with her, an almost adolescent, haphazard rush. But when the clouds of sexual tension and soul-crushing want settled, I was left with the reality of it all.

This wasn't practical. This wasn't appropriate, or even fair. Not to my family, not to Charlie. Not to anyone. I'd remind myself constantly that what I felt with Charlie was no more than a chemical reaction—a release of dopamine and serotonin that left me feeling like I could do anything. That chemical dumping, which we call "love," is really no different than any other chemical dependence. I wasn't weak enough to allow myself to fall victim to narcotics, or even alcoholism. So why couldn't I seem to get enough of the high Charlie left me with?

❖

"You're home late," Peter mumbled as I crawled into bed. I was hoping he would stay asleep. I was hoping I wouldn't have to explain.

"We had a lot to go over. The test is next week." I'd been lying to so many people, for so long, I'd almost begun to believe the things coming out of mouth. The truth, I had to remind myself, was that Charlie and I had finished studying days ago. She was more than ready, but I wasn't quite ready to let her go yet. Instead, we cooked dinners together. Well, I cooked.

Charlie did the dishes to her favorite Joni Mitchell album as I teased her endlessly for being a fan of such outdated folk music. I'd come up behind her, wrapping my arms around her waist, dressed in nothing but one of her oversized plaid shirts, and she would only last another thirty seconds before turning around and kissing me all the way to the bedroom. "A Case of You" would play over her computer speakers, and a few melted candles burned fresh air and spring around us until we, too, melted into each other.

"You've been spending a lot of time there." I waited for Peter to unleash the jealous fury I often saw when I found myself connecting with someone else. It was his only real downfall. More than once he'd threatened to confront a man who'd approach me on the street for directions, or even his own brother for being too friendly with me. But he never did. When it came down to it, Peter was gentle, and kind. And, as always, his short fuse quickly burnt out, and he softened. "I miss having you around. Sammy misses you."

"Soon. It'll be over soon." I lied again.

❖

I didn't know if Charlie was still sleeping with Michelle. And most of me, the self-preserving part, didn't want to know. Their tryst seemed fairly finished after the shower incident.

But it was hard to miss the way Michelle swept past her, brushing her with her breasts and making sure to put her hands on her whenever plausible. It was hard to miss the way Charlie's face burned a hot red when she did.

It was also hard to miss the fact that Charlie was still free.

And even if she wanted to belong to me, I couldn't be hers.

❖

"You want to come out with us tonight, Natalie?" Callie, the young redhead who'd been with us at Panzinelli's the night Jen caught us in the bathroom there, asked innocently as a group of us wrapped up our day shift in the ED that Saturday.

"I…" But all excuses failed me. "Who's going?"

"Oh, pretty much everyone. Katie, Jen, Meg, Richie, Charlie…" My heart lurched. Of course she'd be going. It was Saturday. Shooters night.

"What about me?" Charlie sauntered up behind me.

"I was just inviting Natalie to the bar with us."

"I'm sure Natalie has better things to do than going out drinking with—"

"I'd love to go." Whose voice was that? What was I doing? This was so many different levels of dangerous.

And then, Michelle approached. "Go where?" she asked coyly.

"Natalie's coming out with us tonight. Isn't that awesome?" Callie sounded like a bird chirping.

I watched with gritted teeth as Michelle slid a not-so-subtle hand up Charlie's back. "Awesome."

I nearly turned around on four different occasions on the drive to Shooters. All I'd have to do was make a U-turn, and it would just be me, my bathrobe, and *The Journal* for the night. But then I'd remember Michelle, her smug smile and pouty lips, her big saucer eyes caked in blue eye shadow, her hands wandering over Charlie's body…And I'd keep driving.

"What kind of pinot do you have?" I asked the round, bearded man behind the bar.

"One kind."

"I'll take it."

He slid the glass of cheap wine toward me, and I took several long, drawn-out gulps.

"Hey, you made it." Charlie nudged me, sneaking up behind me with Michelle and Callie in tow.

"You didn't think I'd wuss out, did you?" We shared a quiet smile just between the two of us.

"Come on, Charlie. Let's go get a table." Michelle grabbed her hand, possessively yanking her away toward the seating area. Charlie glanced back over her shoulder at me with something that looked a little like a cry for help. Or maybe it was just wishful thinking on my end.

"They're cute together." Callie.

I'd almost completely forgotten she was there. I smiled gregariously at her, trying hard to hide my disdain. "Adorable."

Callie and I walked to the table that Charlie and Michelle were patronizing, and the others made their way over to join us.

I'd never been in Shooters, but somehow, it was every bit the dive I'd imagined. Northwood didn't have much in the way of hangouts, especially for the college-aged crowd. The walls were an off-white, taking on shades of cigars that had been smoked there for decades. The carpet was a candy red that looked like something you'd find in a bad Chinese take-out restaurant. And young frat boys with scrappy beards spilled their Budweisers on stained pool tables.

I was right on the cusp of looking ridiculously out of place. But my tight jeans and black jacket held me back a half a decade or so, offering a disguise for the discomfort I was feeling. I was sitting on a stool next to Callie and Meg, fiddling with a cocktail napkin in front of me as they endlessly discussed the latest hospital gossip. If they only knew…

"Natalie, come play," Charlie called from the nearby pool table. She leaned against it, her ankles hitched together, the cue resting effortlessly in her hand. She wore a slightly wrinkled flannel shirt that hung loosely on her perfect body, open at the neck just enough to show off the medallion dipping across her chest. Black jeans hugged her straight hips in ways that made me shift uncontrollably in my seat. She really had no idea what she did to me.

"I'm pretty bad," I answered coolly.

"Join the club."

"Maybe in a little bit. I'm going to get another drink."

"Good idea. I'll come with. Here, Michelle, can you hold this?" Without waiting for a response, Charlie thrust her pool cue into Michelle's free hand, never taking her eyes off me.

"Charlie!"

"Go ahead, take my shot for me," she called to her with a smile, and trotted after me like a puppy. As I turned my back to the group, I couldn't help but smile to myself.

"What are you drinking?" she asked with a grin, placing a warm hand on my lower back.

"Pinot. But let's make it a vodka and tonic this time."

"Harry." Charlie hailed the scrappy bartender. "A beer for me, and a vodka soda for the lady." The two quickly performed what looked to be some kind of secret handshake, but her free hand never left my back.

"Coming right up, Charlie."

"The lady? What is this, 1955?" I teased her as I turned to face her.

"Oh, you mean the year you were born?"

"You're cute." I gently brushed the hair away from her eyes as she leaned in toward me.

"Prove it."

With a sweep of the room, I looped my arm through hers and led her back out the door and outside. I hardly made it around the corner before shoving my hands in her back pockets and pushing her against the brick wall. I kissed her fiercely, touching her anyplace I could reach. "I hate when she flirts with you like that," I blurted out after finally coming up for air.

"Good." She kissed me again.

"You love this." I scoffed, pulling away from her grip.

"Well, I don't see you complaining either."

"No. Not this. This! You love it when she flirts with you. Because you love to see me squirm."

"Why, I never." She chuckled and took me in her arms.

"Don't even try to play dumb with me, Charlie Thompson. You love it when I'm jealous. You bastard." I pushed her gently.

"So do something about it."

The air was damp and cold in the wake of a recent rain shower, and I shivered slightly under the dim streetlights coming from Shooters' parking lot. "What do you mean?"

"You know what I mean."

"You know I can't—"

"Then you aren't allowed to get jealous anymore. Come on. Let's go back inside."

She was right. I was already calling all the shots. My selfishness suddenly appalled me. I had no claim on Charlie. I only wished I could convince my heart of that too.

CHAPTER FIFTEEN

It had been a particularly brutal night shift, and by noon, I was still sleeping so deeply I almost missed the loud rapping at the front door. Our nanny had taken Sammy to the pond nearby to feed the ducks, and I was left by myself for a few well-needed moments of rest.

"Hold on," I shouted, throwing on a robe as I ran down the stairs.

"I want a decision." Charlie stood in the doorway, hands placed firmly in her pockets, a black wool cap covering her short hair.

"Excuse me?" I stuttered, reluctantly opening the door and motioning her inside.

"I want a decision. It's me or Peter."

"Charlie. You can't just show up here and demand that I leave my family."

"Not your family," she said, taking one of my hands in hers. "Just him. I want you to choose me, be with me. Don't make yourself miserable anymore. I can see it all over your face. You're killing yourself in this house. And for what? Sammy's sake? Don't you think she's going to figure it out? Don't you think it's worse for her to grow up with a mother who doesn't love her father?"

"Don't talk to me about my daughter!"

"You're right. I'm sorry. Sammy's not my business." Charlie

took a few wounded steps away from me as I sat down at the kitchen table, suddenly overwhelmed with exhaustion. "Sammy is not my business," she said. "But you are, Natalie. Because I love you. And I know, as hard as it is for you to cope with, you love me too. For a year now, you've had it both ways. You've had Peter to come home to at night—the convenience of a husband and a comfortable life with your family. And you've had me. You've had all the passion and excitement and love and lust and whatever else you wanted with me. But I can be that other piece too. I can be the one you come home to. You can have it all."

My stomach turned with anger and fear. "What are you saying?"

"I'm saying this is finished. I won't be your escape from your problems anymore. I won't be here for you whenever it's convenient. I want you, and I want all of you. And I'm done settling for less than that."

"Is this some kind of ultimatum?"

"Yeah," she said firmly, taking a step toward me. "Yeah. I guess it is."

I was silent for a long time, searching futilely for the words to keep my perfectly balanced house of cards from tumbling to the ground. I was seconds away from losing Charlie—unless I was willing to lose Peter. "So you want me to choose, do you?"

"Yes. I want you to choose."

"What do you think I'm going to say? That I'll divorce Peter and run off with you? That's not how this is going to go, and you know it. You've always known that. There was never going to be a happily-ever-after for us. It was fun. And yes, I love you. What I felt was real, I don't doubt that. But if it comes down to my family…my life…then I choose them. Every time."

Charlie said nothing but stared at me hard, walked slowly to me, and kissed me gently on the top of my head in a way that reminded me, distantly, of my mother.

"Good-bye, Natalie."

I stood in front of her, my feet frozen in place. This couldn't be our ending. This couldn't be the fate I'd written for us. I wanted to run after her. I wanted to tell her I loved her with everything I had. I wanted to tell her my fears and my pain and all the ways she'd changed me. But I didn't. I just stood there, watching her go.

❖

"What's the matter with you, kiddo?" Tim asked.

"What are you talking about?" I sat listlessly at my desk, staring blankly at the same head CT I'd been looking at for hours.

"I'm quite sure that room 3's head CT can't be that interesting. It's negative, by the way."

"Yeah, Tim, thanks. This isn't my first day on the job."

"Then stop acting like it. You've been walking around here with your head in the clouds for a week now. Your charting sucks. You're missing things, Natalie. Big things."

My heart sank like an anchor in my chest, and my cheeks burned. "You're checking up on my charts? I'm not a resident anymore."

"Then stop acting like one. And listen. While we're talking, there's something I need to bring up. People have been saying things."

"What kind of things?"

"About you. Things about you possibly being involved too, uh, personally, with a coworker."

"What? That's ridiculous and you know it!"

"Is it? I don't know, kid. It's not my business. But if it is true and it gets back to administration, or anyone else really, you could be in deep trouble. I'd hate to see anything happen to you. You're a great doctor. We both know that."

"Tim," I snarled defensively, "you know people talk."

"Yes. They do. Just keep your nose clean, okay?"

Tim was right. From Charlie's last good-bye, and every day beyond, I'd been essentially among the dead. My patients were receiving mediocre care. My colleagues were picking up my slack. And at home, I'd essentially isolated myself from Peter. On my days off, I'd find perpetual excuses to go to the grocery store, the park, the library—anywhere I could take Sammy to get out of that house. And on the occasions that I did attempt, on some level, to get close to Peter, I failed miserably. I'd made a decision, the decision, although, in reality, I never really had a choice to make.

I'd thought about it, of course—weighed my options carefully. But every scenario played out the same in my head; if I left, I would lose everything: my house, half of my income, and, most devastating of all, Sammy. I could only imagine how the courts would perceive an adulterous, middle-aged lesbian who abandoned her doting husband and disabled child. I could only imagine how anyone would perceive me. Losing Sammy—that was never an option.

And then I would allow myself, at times, to ponder the more optimistic of outcomes. Into my head would come images of a three-bedroom condo by the water, where Sammy would spend most of her time. She would play in the sand, and Charlie and I would sit on the porch and drink a beer and laugh. And after dinner, Peter would arrive, to take his daughter back to his house. We would chat like old friends. And he would empathize with the heart-wrenching decision I had to make in order to be happy.

Charlie would shake his hand. They might make a joke or two. And after he left, Charlie and I would talk about our days at work, where, of course, she was a resident at some nearby teaching hospital, successful and full of that beautiful youthful energy she possessed. We would go upstairs, where she would kiss me passionately good night and hold me as we fell asleep in our bed to the waves lapping outside the window.

It was a goddamned fairy tale—a fantasy so extreme I felt guilty just indulging in it. But when I did…It was euphoric. And I knew, if the world were different, exactly how I wanted my story to play out.

But the world wasn't different. Republican presidential candidates were currently campaigning on the TV to protect "the sanctity of marriage" in the US, while divorce rates were skyrocketing. And, although change seemed to be peeking around the corner, we were far from a society that embraced the things I was doing.

❖

In college, I had a close friend, Kate, who seemed to date nearly every guy in the freshman dorm. We kept in touch over the years, and somewhere in her early thirties, she confided in me that she'd finally fallen in love. Her name was Jane, and they'd been living together in a small Phoenix apartment for over two years now.

Kate was terrified, not only of what her friends and family would think, but of what the world would think. I held her and told her I couldn't have been any happier for her if I tried. And I meant it.

And over the next decade, I'd carefully watched her love another human being in one of the most intense and deeply founded ways I'd ever seen—far, far deeper than anything I'd ever experienced in my years.

But I also watched her struggle. I listened to her cry over the phone when she finally told her elderly parents and had them condemn her to hell. I listened as she screamed about the people on the street corner who'd shout obscenities whenever she tried to so much as kiss the person she loved good-bye for the day. I saw them fight for the big things—marriage, adoptions, civil liberties. But more than that, I saw them scrounge for what the rest of us consider everyday rights: the basic choice to wear what we want, say what we want, love whomever we want…and not risk our safety or, worse, our pride when we do.

I'd remember Kate and Jane as these fantasies of a life with Charlie would inundate my thoughts.

❖

"I'm flying out to Phoenix for a few days," I said casually, placing my suitcase next to me and looking Peter dead in the face.

"What? What for?"

"Last-minute conference. I'll probably visit Kate and Jane while I'm there too."

"You can't just leave like this without warning. What about Sammy? I'm working now."

"We've got a sitter. I'll be back Thursday, okay? This is important."

Peter looked disgruntled for a moment, and then his face softened in its usual submissive manner.

"Okay. Just be safe, all right?"

It seemed Peter had already resigned to losing me, as if, on some innate level, he already knew he was.

"Always. Tuck Sammy in tight and make sure to let her read *Goodnight Moon* to you before bed. She's really proud to be reading now."

"You're a great mother, Natalie. I hope you know that." Peter gently stroked my cheek as an unwelcome ambush of tears flooded my eyes.

"I have to go. My flight leaves in an hour."

"I love you."

But I was already halfway out the front door.

❖

"Do you ever regret it?" I asked Kate, as the Arizona sun beat down on us through the window of a small coffee shop.

"Regret what?"

"You know, your life. Your choices. All of it."

Kate, sitting across from me, looked momentarily stunned. "Are you writing a book or something?" Her face softened into a consoling smile.

"No. I just…it's important. I need to know."

"What's going on with you?"

"Just answer me. Please."

She sat back in her chair and thoughtfully ran her hands through her short, subtly graying hair. "No. I don't regret any of it. Not a single day."

"Really?"

"Really. And frankly, these were never really choices for me. We can't help who God made us. Now, I grew up just as Catholic as you. And believe me, I fought every day of my adult life to stay on what I'd been taught was the 'right path.' But being with Jane—my sexuality, so to say—I couldn't deny that any more than you could deny that you're a doctor. It's fact. It's who I am. I didn't have a choice."

"But you could have married Phil Hendricks, and had kids, and lived a safe, easy life."

"You know what?" she said with a knowing smile. "I'd trade easy and safe for my own happiness any day of the week."

"When you put it that way…"

"Why are you asking me all this? We've been friends for, what, twenty years now? And you've never really been curious about my personal life."

"I'm in love with a woman." The words tumbled out of my mouth.

I wasn't planning to tell Kate about Charlie. In fact, I'd planned to make it an absolute point not to tell her. I had come to spend time with an old friend, who happened to have some experience in the one area I wasn't such an expert in. And I would go home. But before I could even begin to rein it back in, it had spewed out of me like toxic lava.

"I'm sorry. You're what, now?" Kate's jaw was still hanging slightly, and her eyes were wide with a childlike intrigue.

"Shit. I didn't mean to say that. It just…I guess I haven't really told anyone yet, and it's been going on for a year now and I—"

"A year?! You've been in love with a woman for a year, and you haven't even told me? Me, of all people. Your oldest friend. Your oldest and gayest friend? And you couldn't even make a simple phone call to Phoenix to spill it?" She feigned disdain, but a delighted smile lit up her eyes.

"This isn't funny. This is…horrible. It's been the worst thing that's ever happened to me."

"Really." Kate stared me down skeptically.

"Okay, or maybe it's been the best…God, I don't know! See. This is what the last year of my life has been like. Back and forth. Hot and cold. Yes, I want her more than anything. No, I'm not gay. How could I be? I'm pretty sure I've lost my mind completely."

Kate laughed a hearty, slightly patronizing laugh and put a hand on my shoulder.

"You haven't lost your mind. You're just freaking out."

"See, that's exactly what Charlie said."

"Charlie, huh? Sexy."

"It is." I sighed loudly like the dreamy teenager I was. "She is. I mean…I don't know what I mean anymore. Help me?"

She smiled again, this time in a quiet and almost gentle way. "I can't really help you. So if you flew 2,000 miles for that, I'm sorry. But I can be here for you. And over the next couple of days, while you're here, you have my blessing to be who you are, or who you think you might be. And to talk my ear off about this Charlie until you're a little less confused about everything."

"Thank you. Thank you, thank you, thank you." A tsunami of relief I hadn't felt in a year washed over me.

❖

That night, we sat in their small apartment, Kate, Jane, and I, drinking red wine until a feeling of utter safety replaced any hesitation I'd had.

"So tell me about her," Kate blurted out, placing her empty wineglass on the coffee table and putting a comfortable arm around Jane, sitting next to her.

"Yeah, Nat. It's time to spill," Jane said.

"Come on. We're not in college here."

"So pretend we are."

I poured another glass of wine, took a deep breath, and closed my eyes. "What do you want to know?"

Both of them angled themselves to me like excited adolescents. "Everything. What does she look like?"

I could feel myself begin to brighten as I spoke. "She's shorter, but still a little taller than me. Short, messy, brown hair. Beautiful green eyes that will tell you everything she's thinking and feeling. And a body that just won't quit."

They giggled enthusiastically. "Oh my God. You weren't kidding. You do have it bad."

"What are you talking about?"

"You're in love. That's all there is to it. You're glowing."

"I am not. That's such a cliché."

"You, my friend, are that cliché right now."

They probed me with questions about Charlie until the sun was almost up. How old was she? What did she do for work? Who pursued whom? Did Peter know? And not once did either of them ask what I'd decided to do.

"So here's the really important question," Jane said, in a voice that did little to hide her current state of inebriation. "Have you slept with her yet?"

"JANE!" Kate put her fingers to her lips.

"No, no, it's okay." Clearly, the many glasses of wine had left me uninhibited and liberated. "I'll tell you. I mean, really, this is what girls talk about when they get together, isn't it? Sex?"

"True…" Kate replied.

"So what if it isn't sex with men, exactly?"

"Hey, Janie, I think Nat's drunk."

We simultaneously burst out in laughter.

"So you want to know about the sex, huh?"

"So you're saying there has been sex?"

"Oh, yes, there has been sex. There has certainly been sex." I grinned uncontrollably.

"And? How is it?" Jane asked eagerly.

I paused for a moment, searching for the words to say exactly what I wanted to, as the room moved pleasantly around me. "Fucking phenomenal."

Their mouths gaped open, and laughter once again engulfed the house.

❖

It was nearly light out, and the mood in the apartment had shifted to one of reflection and fatigue.

"What are you going to do?" Kate asked. And sadness smothered me until I couldn't breathe as reality once again took hold.

"I already did it."

"What do you mean?"

"I chose Peter. I told Charlie I couldn't be with her. Ever. Not like that." A part of me expected some kind of reprimand from them for shunning their lives, and for taking the easy way out. But both of them just looked saddened, as Kate put a hand on my knee.

"You know," she said, "it took me three years with Jane before I was finally able to come out, to anyone. Even to myself."

"Really?"

"It's not easy. No one said it would be. But I'll tell you this much," she leaned over and kissed Jane tenderly on her chin, "the payoff is more than worth it."

I fell asleep early that morning, drunk and full of a hope I hadn't felt in ages.

❖

I flew out late that afternoon, slept for a few more hours, and headed into work. It had been weeks since Charlie and I had spoken more than a few passing greetings and the obligated patient consults. But coming in that morning, I felt recharged, as if everything I was seeing was new with possibility. Maybe I could do this. Maybe I could let myself be happy.

"Where is everybody?" I asked, once I'd reached the doctors' area.

"They're all in the back. Some kind of party for Charlie or something," the young girl at the desk answered.

I rushed back to the break room, where most of the staff was standing around the table eating doughnuts and drinking coffee.

"Hey, Natalie!" one of the nurses said. "Come have a doughnut." As she moved toward me, I could clearly see Charlie. She stood at the head of the table, a cup of coffee in one hand, half-eaten doughnut in the other, while a beaming Michelle hung proudly from her arm.

"What's going on in here?" I asked.

"We did it." Charlie gently released Michelle's grip and made her way to me, placing her hands on my shoulders.

"We did what?"

"I'm in. I'm going to Brown."

And for a moment, Michelle and everyone around us disappeared. I'd forgotten that I'd let Charlie go. I'd forgotten that she'd clearly moved on. All that mattered was that Charlie had gotten into medical school. She was going to be a doctor, to do exactly what she was born to do. And I had been a part of that.

"What?! Oh my God." I screamed and threw my arms around her neck, unaware of all present company. She grabbed me hard and swung me around as the room filled with a kind of unusual tension.

"I start in September."

"She's not leaving us just yet," Jen said. "She's stuck here for another six months or so, whether she likes it or not." A couple people in the room hooted.

"Guys, I'm only going to Providence. I'll be back to visit."

"That's what they all say," Jen replied with a smile.

"Oh, she'll be back." Michelle sidled up next to Charlie and put her arms around her waist. "She'll be back, because I'll be here."

Jen furrowed her brow and gave me a look I couldn't quite interpret, as a couple of the other staff quietly nudged each other and whispered. Everyone seemed to see what was happening between the two of them and didn't appear to make much effort to keep it a secret.

Nausea overwhelmed me as Michelle brushed the back of Charlie's hair with her palm—just like I used to.

"Well, hey, congratulations, Charlie." I patted her awkwardly on the shoulder and walked out of the room.

❖

"Brown, huh?" I said, quietly walking up behind Charlie, where she sat at a nearby computer.

"Brown. Who'd have thought?" she said proudly.

"I would have."

"Natalie, I want to thank you. I just don't know how. I never would have even tried to do this if you hadn't pushed me. You believed in me when I couldn't believe in myself. How can I thank you enough?"

I leaned over and whispered softly in her ear. "You've given me more than enough in return."

Then I walked away, leaving her looking bewildered and pained in a way I hoped meant she still wanted me like she used to.

CHAPTER SIXTEEN

To say I wasn't completely fixated on Charlie's upcoming departure to Brown would have been a blatant lie. I spent the next several hours seeing patients, going through the motions, doing what needed to be done—but my head, or, at least my heart, was elsewhere.

It wasn't difficult to picture her future either. I could see her, clearly as any reality, clad in a white coat with an even whiter smile, treating patients—saving lives. And I was elated. But a selfish, unyielding depression quickly followed my elation. Charlie was fulfilling her calling, chasing her dreams. And I was no longer a part of that.

Michelle was as vivacious and beautiful as I'd ever seen her, hanging off Charlie's arm whenever she got the chance, like they were on a red carpet somewhere.

I tried being angry with Charlie—who was she to cast me aside like nothing? But really, I had no one to blame but myself. Admitting I was wrong had never been a regular practice of mine. But that afternoon, I was ready to accept that I'd made a mistake. I wasn't exactly sure what that meant, but I knew, somewhere in me, I'd lost something invaluable.

❖

That afternoon, a young girl named Emma Reed came into my ER. I remember her, and will always remember her, because she was five and looked eerily like Sammy. They shared the same dark, wavy hair and bright blue eyes, but more than that, they seemed to have similar spirits—similar souls.

Emma's mother had brought her in for very routine reasons; she hadn't been eating much for the past week and was unusually tired. Her exam was, essentially, normal, except for a low-grade fever and a fast heart rate—neither of which is particularly unusual in a sick, unhappy child.

I sat at my desk, making quick, mundane notes in Emma's chart, stopping periodically to watch Charlie and Michelle giggle and flirt and swoon like they were the only ones in the department. As I watched, trying to figure out what was happening in Charlie's head, Jen whirled around the corner, pushing the pediatric crash cart.

Of all the equipment in an emergency room, this is the one you hope to never have to use.

Instinctively, I jumped up from my post. "Where are you going with that, Jen?" I tried to keep my tone steady.

"It's the little girl in 5." Her voice was tense with urgency—Emma's room.

Charlie must have been paying closer attention than I'd thought, because she immediately grabbed more supplies and followed us.

On the bed in room 5 lay little Emma, white as the fluorescent lights above her. A half-eaten turkey sandwich was still next to her, and two of the other nurses were already hooking her up to the monitors and listening to her chest.

"What happened?" I asked, the bewilderment surely evident in my words.

"She was just eating," one of the nurses said. "She said she didn't feel well, turned blue, and stopped breathing." Emma's mother, who couldn't have been a minute older than Charlie, had just finished a tearful recollection of the last few excruciating moments and was sobbing wildly in the open doorway.

The monitors showed a quick, steady heartbeat, but I knew that wouldn't last.

"Let's get her tubed," I said.

Keeping calm in an emergency is a skill you have to develop. But I don't think anybody ever becomes skilled in watching a child die.

Charlie was at the head of the bed, preparing medications.

"Here. You should do it," I told her quietly, handing her a breathing tube.

"She's so small…" She was hiding it well, but I'd never seen her so frightened.

"This is going to be you someday. You can do it." I put a gentle, tentative hand on her shoulder. "I'm right here."

It took several unnerving seconds, but Charlie eventually secured the tube.

"Good." I offered her a cordial smile and checked back on the monitors above the now-lifeless Emma's head.

"Let's check a pulse," I ordered.

"I can't find one…" Jen shook violently.

"Start CPR."

And for an hour and a half we pushed on her tiny chest and shocked her still heart, every now and then bringing it back to some semblance of life.

"What did we miss here?" I asked again, to no one in particular, as we struggled to keep Emma with us.

"I thought it was just a GI bug," Charlie mumbled, sounding defeated.

"So did I…"

My shift ended at three that day, but I stayed until Emma was stable enough to be transferred out to a teaching hospital in Boston—the same hospital we often took Sammy to.

As the paramedics wheeled her away, small breathing tube

still in place and face still white as light, I thought about losing Sammy. And I thought about my life so far. What had it been? A career and an amazing little girl I adored. A mediocre marriage built around that little girl, and the stability of that career.

And as I watched Charlie, standing outside Emma's room, with an expression so beaten and broken I wanted to run to her, I thought about losing her as well.

I had already given her up. I had already lost her, but to nothing as permanent as death. And finally, I was able to be angry, even downright furious. Life was fleeting. I, of all people, should have known that. So how could I be so intent on letting Charlie go, hoping for a reunion at a better time? Who could say there would ever be a better time?

A week later, we'd received a beautiful, handwritten card from Emma's mother. It turned out she'd been cursed with a rare, congenital heart defect that we couldn't have found, no matter how hard we looked.

She never made it out of the hospital.

❖

"I know how I can thank you," Charlie said with a smile, walking up to my desk as I finished up Emma's transfer paperwork. She squatted to the ground and spoke softly. "Come over tonight. I'll make dinner. Anything you want."

Charlie was a terrible cook. We both knew this. On the one occasion she'd attempted to make dinner for us, she'd burnt the pasta so severely the upstairs neighbor's fire alarm went off. But I didn't care. The idea of spending an evening with her—even if it was just one more—was enough to fill me with more elation than I had words for.

"I'd like that."

"My place. Seven p.m." She put a hand on the back of my neck and then walked away with that familiar swing in her step that brought me to my knees.

❖

"I need you to order a pizza tonight for you and Sammy," I said to Peter, only moments after I'd walked in the door that evening.

"You're going out again?"

"Staff meeting tonight. It'll be late, I imagine. There's a lot going on this month."

"Who is he, Natalie?" I stopped dead as Peter spoke.

"Who is who, Peter?"

"Who is this guy you're having an affair with?" His tone was sharp and cutting.

"There is no guy." I wasn't lying.

"Bullshit. Look me in the eye and tell me honestly that there is no other man." His face was red and his fists were clenched tight against his thighs. I put my things down again and looked at Peter head-on. "There is no other man in my life."

We stood there for a long time, as he stared at me hard. "Okay. I'm sorry. I believe you. I'm sorry—"

"Don't ever accuse me of that again."

"I won't. I'm sorry. It's just that you've been so distant lately, even for you. And you're gone all the time. This last year, you just haven't been around at all."

"I'm a physician. I'm busy. You knew this when you married me. Now, I have to go. I'm late for my meeting." I picked up my keys and my purse, and walked out the door.

I arrived at Charlie's ten minutes later, bringing along with me a state of unreasonable excitement. I rang the doorbell, thinking that if I wanted to change our situation, I had to change old habits too. My trip to Phoenix had left me with a lot to ponder. It would never be too late for us. And when I was ready, I'd come around. And Charlie would be there.

"It was unlocked, you know," Charlie said, opening the door to greet me. She wore a pair of black slacks, polished dress shoes, a freshly ironed blue button-down shirt, and I instantly wanted her more than I'd ever wanted anyone, or anything.

"You look really nice." I fought the need to undress her right in the doorway.

"Oh, yeah, well, I figured a little ironing doesn't kill anyone." She led me in the house and into the kitchen. I'd been there a hundred times before, but that night, I could hardly recognize the place. Not a single dirty dish was out. The counters were clean. The table was set with matching plates and silverware. Candles lined the room, leaving nothing but a soft, flickering light in the place. And brass instruments hummed jazz music from the nearby stereo.

"Sit down. Let me get you a glass of wine." I was still looking around in awe as Charlie pulled my chair out for me.

"That'd be nice. Thanks."

She poured me a glass of what looked to be fairly expensive pinot and brought it to me at the table. "How does salmon with hollandaise and asparagus sound to you?"

"It sounds like you had some help." I was teasing her, and she laughed with me.

"Yeah. Paula Deen. It's amazing how these science courses have helped me follow a recipe. They say you can't learn anything practical in school. Who'd have known organic chemistry would help me charm women?"

"I don't think you need any help in that area." I grinned suggestively at her and took another sip of my wine, allowing the warmth to envelope me like a blanket.

"It'll be ready in ten minutes or so," she said, pulling up a chair next to me and drinking from her own glass of wine.

"You know you didn't have to go to all this trouble for me."

"I know I didn't. But I wanted to. You've done so much for me, Nat. And I know it'd be easy to be pissed at you, or hurt, or whatever, but I can't."

"You can't?"

"Don't get me wrong. I was pissed about how things ended with us—for a few weeks. I guess I couldn't wrap my head around why anyone wouldn't choose me." She laughed at herself. "Ridiculous, I know. But I guess that's the cocky butch in me."

"I think most people would choose you, Charlie."

"But not you."

"Most people don't have Sammy to think about."

"You know you'd never really lose her. No court is going to take a child away from a mother like you—gay or not. And you know how good I am with her."

"Yes. I realize that." Out of habit I took her hand in mine and placed it on my knee. A familiar shiver of need ran through me as her bare skin touched my leg. "Trust me, Charlie. Don't think I haven't thought of all this. I know how good you are and how much Sammy would love having you around. But what if Peter tried to take her from me?"

"He would never."

"Are you so sure? Because I've been married to him for a while now, and I've seen people do some crazy things when they're hurt. And believe me, this would hurt him. I really don't know what he'd be capable of if he knew about us. I just couldn't risk that."

"Even if he tried, no judge is going to take that little girl away from you. She adores you." Logically, I was sure she was right. I was only prodding deeper for more excuses to keep my life safe and secure.

"How do you do it, Charlie?"

"Do what?"

"Be so damn okay with who you are?"

She finished her wine and squeezed my hand. "It takes time. That's all. Just like anything else."

"You're awfully wise for your age, you know," I said. "Maybe that's why it was so easy to fall in love with you."

The oven timer rang, and shortly thereafter, Charlie brought dinner to the table.

"Better than burnt pasta, huh?" she said with a smile.

"You're just full of surprises, aren't you? You know, I went out to Phoenix to visit a friend from college. A lesbian friend."

"No kidding. Natalie has a dyke friend. Doesn't that sort of disrupt your Stepford Wife image?" She laughed.

"Very funny. Actually, Kate and I have been friends since college. But she didn't come out until she was in her thirties."

"So what happened to her?"

"She's been living happily with her partner for eight years now. And I've never known any two people better suited for each other." We were both quiet for a while. "I went out there mostly because I needed to talk to somebody. About you."

"What for?"

"I've been holding this in for a year now. And the only person who's had any idea is you. Well, you and Jen. Though God knows she's not up for talking about it. But really. It was… enlightening, to say the least."

"How so?"

Did she know where I was going with this? Did I even know?

"I saw Kate and Jane, and their life together. And I saw two people who couldn't love anybody else as much as each other. I saw friendship and respect and affection, and all kinds of things I don't see in my own marriage. Things…things I see with you, Charlie."

"What are you saying?"

I touched her face. "I'm saying I love you, Charlie. I love you more than I even have words for. More than I ever thought I could love anybody in my entire life. You've given everything meaning, where there was none. When you're around, I'm content and euphoric all at once, and not in a fleeting way, either. I love you in a way I'm sure could last." I was drunk, and so was Charlie. The words I spoke were honest, but they were also dangerous. They were the kind of words that required action— action I wasn't yet ready to take.

"I love you too. I've loved you for so long now. But if you aren't ready to leave Peter…"

I took her face in my hands and kissed her with all the passion and urgency that had been building in me since Phoenix.

Charlie grabbed my hips and guided me to a standing position, running her hands down my sides and under my shirt, pulling it away from my body. Her skin was warm, and her lips were soft and wet as they traced eagerly along my neck and down to my breasts. Her fingers skillfully unbuttoned my top, while one hand gently tugged on my loose hair.

"I want you so much," I gasped, as she pushed me onto the table. I pulled my hands through her hair as she kissed down my stomach. My body was lit up. The most visceral parts of me cried out for her to touch me. She bit gently at my bare shoulders as she slid off my bra and smoothed her thumb over my breasts. "God, you know just how to touch me."

Charlie laid me down on the table, taking time and care not to leave a single inch of me untouched or unkissed. Her lips moved fervently against mine, and her tongue gently and masterfully found my mouth. Just kissing her could turn me on like nothing else. I unbuckled her belt and slowly took off her pants, pulling her down on top of me and sliding my hand inside the band of her black briefs. She groaned softly as my fingers found their way to exactly where she needed me.

❖

I was sure I'd fallen asleep for a few minutes, lying there with Charlie collapsed in my arms. It was beautiful to see her so vulnerable, breathing heavily, head tucked under my chin. She was always so strong and in control. Sometimes, it was nice to see her let go a little.

"Charlie," I nudged her, kissing her head, "I have to get going. It's late."

"I know." She pulled on her pants and walked me to the door.

We stood there for what felt like an eternity, just looking at each other, both of us daring the other to make a move. I didn't want to go. I wanted to spend the night with her again. I wanted to wake up in her arms and make her coffee, go off to work together. All at once, I wanted all the little things with her—breakfasts, and holidays, and family vacations, and pictures of us in the living room, and Saturday trips to the store. I wanted to share my life with her, and her with me. I wanted Charlie, in every way. Not just for the night either.

"Look, I don't think that was such a great idea."

My heart fell ten stories. "Why not?"

"A million reasons. You aren't really going to leave Peter. And let's be honest here. Even if you did, you and I could never work, at least not long-term. You may be older than me, but in lesbian years, you're about fifteen."

"What's that supposed to mean?"

"It means we're in completely different places here. You aren't ready to be out yet. And you won't be where I'm at for a long time. That's a problem for me."

"I'm a fast learner. You know that."

"It's not a skill. It's just something you have to go through. Besides, I'm leaving for Brown in a few months. I'll be in med school. I don't have to tell you how little you'll see of me. And it's not like you could move to Providence."

"It's a thirty-minute drive."

"And what happens when I'm in residency? Who knows what part of the country I'll end up in? You can't leave. You have Sammy."

"Don't you think you're getting a little ahead of yourself here? What are you saying, Charlie?"

She took a long, sharp breath and pushed a piece of hair out of my face. "I'm saying it's over."

If I'd ever known real, crushing pain before, it was nothing compared to what I felt in that moment. Not when my father died. Not when patients had died. Not ever. It was as if all at once my world suddenly stopped spinning and everything I'd been hoping for, every chance I thought I'd had at being truly happy, was ripped out from under me without warning. This must be what having your heart broken felt like.

"What's this really about?"

"The truth?"

I nodded.

"I can't keep hurting over you. Sure, tonight you're in love with me. Tonight you're going to leave Peter. But when you go home and you kiss that perfect little girl good night, you'll never be able to leave. I'll never have you. And I have to start accepting that. No more sex on the kitchen table. No more kissing in the dark. None of it."

"So what?" I said bitterly. "You're just going to run off to Brown now and be with Michelle?"

"What does Michelle have to do with this?"

"You tell me. You two were awfully close at work earlier."

She laughed at me. "You don't get to care. You don't get to have it both ways anymore. I know I said that a few weeks ago, but I mean it now. I have to mean it. You won't leave your husband. You won't be honest with yourself about who you are. And you don't get to care who I'm going to be with."

"Charlie…"

"What? What could you possibly have to say that you haven't said a hundred times before?"

I stood, awestruck, as I realized, there was, in fact, nothing left to say.

"That's what I thought," she said, opening the door to let me out. "Good-bye, Natalie."

Not knowing what else to do, I silently walked out into the cold night.

CHAPTER SEVENTEEN

Charlie was right. I wasn't going to leave home. I wasn't ready to be honest with myself. And as I kissed Sammy good night that night, I knew that. Even if it meant sacrificing my own happiness indefinitely.

I went into work the next morning to find an email from the director of the emergency department. It was simple and to the point.

As of today, Charlie Thompson will no longer be working at Northwood. We wish her luck as she ventures onto Brown's medical school in the fall.

I stared at the computer screen for a long time, willing the message to change. But it didn't. And as the reality of it all sank in, I was surprised to feel hot tears fill my eyes. I would never work with Charlie again. And it was likely, more than likely actually, that she would manage to disappear from my life for good.

I was selfish enough to believe I was the cause of her departure—especially given the previous night's exchange. Maybe I was right, but I had to find out. Rumors were circulating like a head cold. Some of them said she'd been fired for her relationship with Michelle. Some of them said she'd quit after a fight with the manager. And one or two said she was having an affair with one of the hospital physicians.

"Why'd she do it?" I snarled, cornering Michelle in the trauma room.

"I don't know. I thought you might."

"Me? Why would I know? You're her girlfriend."

She snickered at me. "Girlfriend? Hardly. I've been working on that for almost a year now. But Charlie's only got eyes for our favorite doctor."

Heat crawled into my face and my heart leapt into my throat. "What are you talking about?"

"You two."

"Charlie told you."

"Never. She'd never put you in jeopardy like that. But I'm not stupid, Natalie. I see the way you two look at each other. The way you smile when you pass each other in the halls. Your little study dates at her place. You think you're so subtle. But it's plain as shit. No. Charlie never wanted me. She's in love with you."

"Does anybody else know?"

"No. I don't think so. Although that little embrace in the break room yesterday probably didn't help things much."

My face flushed again. "Please. Don't tell anyone."

"Why would I start now?"

I nodded gratefully and started to leave the room.

"Oh, Natalie?" I stopped and turned. "One more thing. You're a smart doctor. And as much as I want Charlie, I've always liked you. But I'll be damned if you aren't stupid as hell for letting that girl walk out of your life."

I returned to my desk and picked up the phone, eyeing the patient census to make sure I wasn't neglecting my work. Charlie's voice mail picked up after a single ring.

"Charlie. It's me. I heard. But why? I know you weren't fired. No one here would dream of that. But why would you leave? Think about your career. Think about me. Call me. Okay? Soon?"

I hung up and quickly sent her a text message from my cell phone.

Call me. Want to know you're okay.

The day trudged on, as I tried to focus on my patients and the medicine in front of me. But in the back of my mind, all I could do was wonder about Charlie. The idea of never seeing her again—as if she'd just died—was so overwhelming at times, I almost couldn't breathe. But I'd remember my training and submerge myself in my work, in one of the only things on earth I loved almost as much as I loved her.

By the end of the day, I still hadn't heard from her. And the rumor mill was starting to quiet down a bit. Most would forget about Charlie after a few weeks and go on with their jobs and their lives. I was certain I would not be among them. There were no emails. No phone calls. No texts returned.

A week passed where I heard nothing. Each day I'd expect to see her swing through the ER doors, bag on her shoulder, wool cap on her head, confidence in her step. But she never did. And eventually, the hospital hired someone else—a young guy who wasn't nearly as good as Charlie, or as well liked.

❖

Last summer had blitzed us like a sniper. And the mild Rhode Island winter seemed to skip spring and suddenly turn into a blistering heat you'd only find in August. It was July, though, and not a single day passed that I didn't hope I'd somehow run into Charlie. The truth was, I had no idea where she was or what she was doing. It was possible, likely even, that she wasn't even in Northwood anymore. My attempts to reach out to her had gone unanswered. She was gone.

❖

I sat by the water one afternoon, watching Sammy run in the tide and throw handfuls of sand at the seagulls. And like a dream, or a memory, I thought about Charlie and the fairy-tale fantasy I'd had of what our lives together could have been, if the world had been perfect. No—if I had been brave.

A warm, mid-summer rain drizzled from the sky as I packed up Sammy and her things and headed toward the car. As I walked, an emptiness like I'd never felt before overwhelmed me. An emptiness I knew would never be filled if I continued living the life I was in. As we pulled into the driveway, my heart sank farther toward my feet. I didn't dread anything more than coming home to Peter.

"How was the beach?" he asked as we came through the door.

"It was fun," Sammy, no longer a young child, said with a smile.

"Good. Spaghetti for dinner." He hugged her and leaned in to kiss me. I pulled away, as I'd done every time since Charlie's departure. As if the distance between Peter and me hadn't been obvious enough, Charlie's absence only increased it tenfold. Peter and I hadn't made love in months. In fact, I hadn't even allowed him to touch me. I never stopped to wonder if he'd noticed. I guess I didn't really care.

"Sammy, go play in your room for a while. I want to talk to Mommy. We'll call you when dinner's ready." Sammy obeyed and ran off toward her room with her pile of books.

"What is it, Peter?"

"You tell me."

"Tell you what?" The last thing I wanted to do was discuss our marriage.

"Do you even want to be married to me anymore?"

His words bowled me over like a train. "I'm sorry?"

"You heard me."

My pulse bounded in my neck and my head swam. "Honestly? I don't know, Peter."

"Why? What happened to us?" He sat down at the nearby table and sunk his head into his hands.

"I don't know," I said, sitting down next to him.

"Well, you have to know something." He no longer sounded angry.

"I've been having these thoughts…these feelings…"

"Thoughts? Feelings? About who?"

I hesitated again and turned to face the wall. I'd never consciously decided to leave him. I'd resigned myself to a life of mediocrity and only mild truthfulness. But the words kept tumbling out of my mouth like a landslide. "Charlie Thompson."

"Charlie Thompson? Wait, the medic? But she's a…"

"Woman. Yeah, Peter. I know."

"I don't get it," he said, shaking his head. "You're a… lesbian?"

"Yes. I don't know. Maybe?"

"How long has this been going on?"

I thought for a moment. "Eighteen, nineteen months or so?"

"Are you fucking kidding me?"

"Peter, I'm sorry." But I wasn't as sorry as I thought I should have been.

That night, I packed a bag and stayed with Tim and his wife. As I sat awake in the guest room, I thought about Sammy and what it would be like to have her only half the time. But Peter was a wonderful father, one of the best. I couldn't take her from him. As if I wasn't being selfish enough, I now had to start contemplating leaving my child fatherless?

It would be years before I could forgive myself for leaving.

Another part of me, though, went beyond the guilt and self-loathing. This part was overcome with a sense of reprieve. I could start over. I could build the life I'd always wanted but never allowed myself to dream of. For the first time in a decade, I was alone. It was frightening but also exhilarating. And I couldn't shake the feeling that nearly anything could happen next. I could have the job, and the house, and the perfect child, and the perfect partnership. I could have it all.

But I couldn't have Charlie. If I'd only been stronger, maybe it wouldn't have been too late. Maybe we'd be together, in a life where I didn't have to settle for good enough anymore. I'd never know, though, because I hadn't been stronger and Charlie was gone.

If I'd managed to sleep at all that night, I would have dreamt of Charlie. Instead, I settled for broken, tortured fantasies, my favorite of which involved walking out of the hospital into the warm, summer night, to find her leaning up against my Jeep.

She's wearing her leather jacket, and her bike is parked next to her. With her arms folded across her chest, she stands and smiles at me silently.

"Charlie?" I call to her.

She looks older, more certain of everything. She doesn't answer at first but continues to smile at me. As I start to move faster, she motions for me to come closer to her. I do. Without saying anything, she takes my face in both of her strong, overworked hands, softly at first, and looks at me carefully. Her smile deepens, and my pulse is rushing in my ears. It's dark, but the neon light from the nearby EMERGENCY sign is enough to highlight the lines that form around her eyes when she laughs.

She kisses me until I'm so dizzy I can hardly stand anymore, but she doesn't stop. Instead, she instinctively holds me by the shoulders, controlling every aspect of the moment.

"I heard about Peter. I'm sorry," she says.

"Don't be."

"I'm proud of you, Natalie."

"Charlie, I love you."

She kisses me again. This time with even more energy and passion, until I think I may disappear into the night.

"I'm leaving for Brown next week."
"I know."
"You know, someone once reminded me that's only thirty minutes from Northwood."
I laugh lightly.
"I want you, Natalie. All of you. Be with me. No more holding back. No more secrets. Just us."

And I throw my arms around her neck in wordless approval until the darkness of reality swarms in and the fantasy fades to a sleepless dream.

CHAPTER EIGHTEEN

By mid-August, Peter and I had worked out a makeshift custody agreement that allowed us to share our time in the house, to save Sammy the confusion of bouncing back and forth. He was hurt and angry and mystified as to what had gone wrong between us. But he was also civil—due mostly, I'm sure, to the beautiful child we had together. However, none of this surprised me. Peter was a decent man, so I would do anything in my power to be as accommodating as possible.

Still, I was lonely. Beyond lonely, really. When I wasn't in our Beech Street home, I was renting a small cottage near the ocean, where I made it a point to work more than I'd ever worked in my life. In my worst moments, I'd begin to dial Charlie's number, knowing full well she would never pick up. But pride and maybe rationality would kick in, and I'd hang up before the phone ever had a chance to ring. Then I would go back to futile attempts to drown in research and patient charts and the more-than-occasional glass of wine.

One particularly excruciating day, I drove to the bookstore and bought a piece of fiction that centered on two women and their relationship together. I was instantly captivated by their companionship and the power between them, in spite of the fact the book was poorly written lesbian beach reading. But by the second or third chapter, I noticed that the place in me that burned so strongly for Charlie was only further ignited, until I was so desperate for her I couldn't sit still anymore. Eventually, I realized I was doing nothing but torturing myself.

I made my way to the kitchen trash, holding the book over it. But a part of me thought better and tucked it away behind some old editions of the *Journal of Medicine* I knew I'd never touch again. Just in case. In case of what, I wasn't sure. But just in case.

Once in the bedroom of the tiny cottage, I stared in the vanity mirror for so long I almost didn't recognize myself. This wasn't me. It wasn't the first time during the last year or two I'd had this thought. But I wasn't debating my sexuality this time. No. This was about self-pity. I was a problem solver, not someone who sat around bathing in misery until they simply melted into a pile of despair. It was time to pick up and move on. Charlie was gone. I'd missed my chance. Or maybe we'd missed our chance together.

And suddenly, with this epiphany, came another stronger, more pleasant need. I needed to be with a woman. Maybe I wouldn't find another Charlie right away. Maybe I never would. But that night, I needed that companionship. I needed that power, even if it was just a fraction of what I'd lost.

I brushed out my hair, put on a little more mascara, and changed out of my sweatpants, trying to find something in my closet that would give me enough confidence to even flirt with another woman. I didn't know if I could do it. But I did know I couldn't spend one more night alone by the water.

❖

It didn't take long before someone approached me. She was tall, maybe five-eight, with long blond hair and a tattoo on her right clavicle. I couldn't quite gauge how old she was—forty? forty-five? Certainly my age, looking a little worse for it. She wasn't terribly unattractive, and three shots deep, I thought about going back to her place for the night. But as we spoke, I couldn't get past the fact she was uneducated and pluralized words like "somewhere" and "anywhere." She also had a sort of feminine softness that Charlie didn't possess, one that felt more like weakness than anything else to me. It did nothing for my libido.

As I sent her away, I realized I wasn't even out yet and had already managed to develop a type. I liked androgyny, "butch," as Charlie called herself, although I always thought that had sort of a negative connotation outside of the gay community. I loved her masculine strength, her old world-chivalry, the way she opened doors and gave me her jacket. Her strong jaw, her soft eyes that allowed a look into her soul, her stubbornness and her strength—all of it was balanced by a femininity that allowed her to know herself—her feelings—and make it a point to know me, in every way she possibly could.

I'd developed a preference. Not even a preference, but a necessity. If I was going to be with a woman, she'd have to be this kind of woman.

"I'm sorry. I'm straight and in the middle of a divorce," I told the tall blonde, learning quite quickly that gay women, naturally drawn to drama, hate this kind of thing. Most of them aren't looking to be a heartbroken straight woman's one-night experiment. She walked away without a fight, and I was once again alone, in the most popular gay bar in Providence.

It was only eleven thirty p.m., and my head was swimming from shots of Grey Goose. The tall blonde had found someone else to prey on, near the pool tables, and I was having trouble finding a single person there I might even be able to fake it with for a night. This was a lost cause. Alone, discouraged, and far too drunk to drive back to Northwood, I contemplated my next move.

"I'll close my tab now," I told the spiky-haired young woman tending the bar.

I signed the bill as quickly as my blurry eyes allowed and headed toward the door. A crowd had formed outside, mostly women, mostly coupled up with other women, but I didn't take the time to look closely as I pushed past them.

"Excuse me." I slurred my words carelessly as I made my way through them. "Excuse me. Just trying to leave."

Someone I couldn't see grabbed my arm hard.

"What the fuck!" I turned quickly, ready to unleash my night of pathetic failure and months of sexual frustration on the next person to cross my path.

"Natalie." I knew that voice from my past. But mostly, I knew it from every dream I'd had since.

But when I looked around, I didn't see her anywhere. And the hand that had gripped my arm had been pushed away by someone trying to make their way to the door. Could I have had so much to drink I was hallucinating? Maybe the tall blond woman had slipped me something. Or maybe I'd already passed out at home, and this was nothing more than another unsolicited excursion into a fairy tale I'd never live.

"Natalie." This time the voice was louder and more commanding—almost angry. She emerged from the tangled mess of people. "Natalie? What are you doing?"

I said nothing, but fell gracelessly into Charlie's arms. "OhmygodCharlie," I finally shouted.

"You're drunk."

"A little…" I mumbled into her shoulder. The scent of her cologne and the feeling of her body against mine sent a familiar chill through me, as I continually monitored the reality of the moment.

"You're drunk. Beyond drunk, actually. In Providence. At a gay bar."

"And you're observant." I laughed a little and put a sloppy hand to her cheek. "I'm so happy you're here, Charlie."

"Natalie. Look at me." Through closed eyes, I felt her take me by the shoulders and hold me in front of her. "What are you doing here? Is everything okay?"

"I'm here because I couldn't be alone one more second. And I guess a gay bar seemed like an appropriate place to pick up a girl for the night?"

"You're cruising a lesbian bar. You. That's what you're telling me."

"Sure is."

"Where's Peter? And Sammy?"

"At their house." Charlie slipped her arm around me and guided me out of the crowded line to her car.

"You can't drive back to Northwood. You're a train wreck."

"I'm a doctor. I can do whatever I like."

"We're not at work. Now get in the car. I'm taking you to my place."

"I've waited months to hear those words from you."

❖

When I woke up I wasn't sure what time it was or what had happened. I searched my surroundings through the dim morning light, realizing I didn't know where I was either. My head pounded as I rolled over and buried my face in the strange couch cushions, as pieces of the evening before slowly presented themselves.

"Drink this," Charlie said, walking out of the kitchen holding a mug. She was standing in front of me, wearing nothing but boxer briefs and a tank top. Her hair was particularly disheveled in a way that instantly reminded me of the first day in the on-call room. And as terrible as my body told me to feel, I was thrilled to have woken up near her.

"Nice place," I said with a smile, examining the mug she handed to me.

"It's just coffee. Black and strong. I haven't forgotten." She took a seat on the couch next to me.

"Thanks. So this is home now?"

"This is it. For the next four years of my life or so."

"When does school start?"

"Two weeks. But listen, I don't want to talk about med school right now."

I took a long, comforting sip of my coffee and rested my head on my free hand. "Okay. So what do you want to talk about then?"

"You. What were you doing at Gallery last night?"

"Drinking too much."

"Natalie. I'm serious."

I sucked in a deep breath, trying to focus through the pain in my head. "I left Peter."

Charlie was silent as she stared at me for so long I had to wonder if time had stopped completely. "You did?"

"Yes. Last month."

"Wow. I'm not going to lie. I never thought we'd be having this conversation. Did you tell him? About us, I mean?"

"I told him everything."

She was quiet again, this time more reflective than anything else. "And Sammy?"

"She's fine. Right now, we're sharing our time at the house. Peter has her Monday through Wednesday and every other weekend. I have a little cottage by the water, and he's staying with his brother in town when he's not there. And Sammy seems none the wiser, really, although I'm sure she can tell something's going on."

"And you? Are you all right?"

"Well," I said thoughtfully, "right now, I'm hung over like a frat boy."

"You know what I mean." She reached over and rubbed my back. "Are you okay? You know, with all of this."

"Yes. Yes, I really am. It's hard being away from Sammy, that's true. And it's strange being on my own again. But I'm happy. I'm happier without him." And I meant it.

"So does this mean you're admitting you might be, you know, one of us?"

I laughed at her subtlety. "I might be. But I'm not exactly attending pride parades or anything quite yet."

"You know," she said, taking my hand, "coming out isn't an event. It's not something you wake up one day and decide to do. It's a process. It happens slowly, over time. Maybe the first step was leaving home. Now you just have to work on being okay with you. No matter who that ends up being."

I collapsed back onto the couch as Charlie picked up both of my legs and laid them over her lap, covering them with a fleece blanket. "Did you really put me on your couch last night?"

She smiled. "Where was I supposed to put you? On the floor?"

"Your bed?"

"Have I ever been anything but chivalrous?"

"Never. How'd you get me up here anyway?" I asked, noting the two stories below us.

"Fireman's carry."

"You're kidding, right?"

"How else did you think I did it? We didn't have any elevators handy."

"So you just picked me up, put me over your shoulders, and carried me up two flights of stairs."

"Yeah. They should really call it the paramedic's carry, now, huh?"

"Well, I'm certainly embarrassed." I laughed.

"Don't be. First gay-bar experience, you get a free pass."

"How about you?" I asked, tentatively. "Anyone in your life these days?" I wasn't sure I wanted to know the answer.

"Just a girl here and there. Nothing worth mentioning though."

A sense of relief found me, until I began to dwell on what the "here and there" meant. Girls in Charlie's bed, in her arms. Kissing her, touching her, knowing her. And a burst of possessive energy came over me so strongly I had to fight the urge to hold on to her with everything I had.

"What are you going to do now?" she asked.

"What do you mean?"

"I mean, with your life? With yourself? Everything."

"Exactly what I've been doing. Keep trying to figure it all out, I guess."

We fell silent again, as I reached out and ran my fingers through her hair. Touching her again was like finding water during a drought. I watched as her eyes closed involuntarily, momentarily giving in to what I knew she was still feeling for me.

"So are you going to explain, Charlie?"

"Explain what?"

"Oh, I don't know. Abandoning your job? Your life?"

"You mean abandoning you?"

I turned away from her abruptly. "Well, yes, that too."

"That night," she said, facing me pensively, "I knew it was over between us. For good." My stomach tossed and turned viciously. "And I couldn't imagine coming into that ER day after day and facing you, looking at you, knowing I could never have you the way I wanted. So I called Maria and told her I had personal reasons I couldn't disclose, and I had to resign."

"And that was it? You just gave up everything in your life and fled to Providence?"

"Pretty much, yes. I did what I had to do to protect myself. I couldn't look at you every day and know you were going home to him."

"I'm not anymore." I softly ran my fingertip along her jaw and watched as she melted into my touch.

"No. No, you're not." She sat motionless as I leaned toward her and slowly kissed her.

"Natalie, stop," she said tenderly, pulling away.

"What? Why?"

"How did you think this would go? You'd leave your husband, and four weeks later you'd come find me, and we'd fall passionately into each other's arms and live happily ever after?"

"Well, kind of! What are the chances we would run into each other last night? It was meant to happen." I was whining.

"Even if that were true…There's so much more to it than that."

"Like what? I know you still love me. And God knows I'm still so in love with you, Charlie. You're all I've thought about for months now. When you left, my world fell apart. No one has ever had that kind of effect on me before. Ever."

"I do love you. I won't deny that. But nothing is that simple. You're in the middle of a complicated divorce. You've got Sammy to think about. I start medical school in two weeks. I live here. You live there. And you're just starting to come to terms with the fact that you want to be with a woman. You know how long that takes to deal with?"

"We can do it. Together. We can be together. I can visit on the weekends. Hell, I can even help you study."

"And what? We'll sleep in my twin bed next to my empty beer-bottle collection?"

"Yes! If that's what it takes. Okay, maybe not that. But we'll get you a new bed. Whatever we have to do."

"You're crazy."

"Charlie, look at me," I said, suddenly fierce, and grabbed her strong shoulders, "I want this. And you know I won't quit until I get my way. I'll fight for you."

"You know something?" she said, laughing softly to herself. "I've waited over a year to see you fight for me. I never thought I would. But now that I have, I'm not so sure—"

"I know you aren't just some young kid who wants something until it's theirs. What we have is real. And you damn well know it."

"That's not it. I want you. I'll never deny that. And I'm beyond thrilled that you finally want me back, just as much. But I'm scared."

"You aren't scared of anything."

"That's not true." She laughed again. "I'm scared of heights.

Med school. And spiders. And I'm scared as hell of losing you again."

I felt my face soften into a sympathetic, doting smile, and I took her in my arms. "I'm not stupid enough to push you away again."

"What about Peter? What if you decide to go back to him? What if you can't handle this life?"

"There are always going to be what-ifs. You know that. But I will promise you this much. I will never go back to Peter. And I will try with everything I have in me to make this work between us. And you know I don't like failure."

"I don't know, Natalie."

❖

After a long, sobering shower, I walked out in nothing but my towel and a small, knowing grin.

Charlie jumped from the couch and covered her eyes. "Jesus. If you're going to hang out here, you have to wear clothes."

"I have no idea what you're talking about," I said simply, letting the bath towel slip a little bit more.

"You're not as innocent as you want to come off, you know."

"Maybe not." I walked slowly toward her, stopping just close enough that I could feel her hot breath on me. "But it sure is fun to watch you squirm."

Charlie sucked in a hard, fast breath and closed her eyes again, appearing to will herself to stay put. "I can't sleep with you," she said firmly.

"That's really too bad." I moved closer, until our bodies were touching just slightly, and let go of the towel. "Whoops."

I took a step back and watched as she stared me down from my head, to my feet, and back up again.

"That's fighting dirty."

"So what are you going to do about it?"

Her eyes twinkled with challenge and a waning restraint as she put her hands on my naked hips and pushed me hard onto the couch. I giggled with pleasure as I pulled my fingers through her hair.

"You know just how to push all my buttons, don't you," she said, propping herself up with one arm and touching the length of my body with her free hand.

"I love you, Charlie. I want this. I want you."

"You really think we can make this happen?"

"Yes. I really do."

She kissed me long and tenderly, stroking my hair and rubbing my naked stomach. "You really want to be with me," she said, stopping abruptly.

"Yes. That's what I'm telling you."

"So prove it."

"What?" I sat up and pulled my knees to my chest. "How?"

"A dry run."

"What are you talking about?"

"A dry run. Stay with me until tomorrow. We'll go out to dinner. We'll wander the city. We'll do what any other couple would do."

"So, you want to date me?"

"Exactly."

"And if we pass the dry run?"

She ran her fingers down my spine, forcing every part of my body to tremble.

"If we pass the dry run," she whispered, and kissed my earlobe, "then we get to keep doing it over and over again."

"Deal." And we continued to kiss, for so long I lost track of time, and place, and interest in anything but the moment at hand.

❖

"You ready to go?" Charlie said, coming out of the bathroom holding her toothbrush.

"Just waiting for you." I smiled at her. She stood in front of me wearing a pair of dark jeans and a tight, black T-shirt, looking every bit the biggest part of all of my sleeping and waking dreams of the past year. She held out her hand for me to take, and I did, as she led me out of her apartment and into the warm, late-summer afternoon.

We lay on a blanket in a nearby park, drinking iced tea and studying the clouds.

"When is the divorce final?" Charlie asked.

"Another month or so, if everything goes like it's supposed to."

"How's Peter handling everything?"

"He's doing all right. Angry, I don't doubt. But he hides it well. All he's really said about it since I left was 'I hope you're taking care of yourself, Natalie.'"

"He's a good guy."

"Unfortunately, I think it was the 'guy' part that ruined things."

We laughed hard.

"God, Natalie. I never thought I'd live to see the day where you even breathed the word 'gay.' I have to say, it's pretty great."

"James Pratt. Remember him?"

"Hypothermia kid. The one you saved. How could I forget?"

"That day, watching you work on him—the grace you carried yourself with, the strength, the sheer, I don't know, sex appeal that you brought with you in a crisis…I knew that day that you were trouble." I smiled, warmed by the memory. "I knew there was something about you I couldn't stay away from. And when you kissed me that day—"

"You mean when you pinned me in the on-call room and made me kiss you?"

"That's exactly what I mean. From that second forward, you had me more than you ever realized."

Charlie turned over and kissed my neck. "Now I just have to figure out how to keep you."

CHAPTER NINETEEN

A s if it were possible to think about Charlie any more than I already had been, I spent the next five days in Northwood counting down my next weekend with her like a child waiting for Christmas. Work was a welcome distraction, but in the back of my mind, I was giddy with the anticipation of seeing her again— of being hers.

That Friday evening, I finished up with my last patient and took off without so much as changing my clothes.

"You're the most gorgeous thing in scrubs I've ever seen," Charlie said with a smile as she met me at the door.

"Are you ever not excruciatingly charming?" I threw my arms around her neck and kissed her until my legs began to shake.

"Never."

❖

We sat on her tiny porch with the chipped railing, drinking hot coffee and watching the sun set on the first real day of fall Rhode Island had seen that year. The leaves had just barely begun to turn, and trees were painted with deep orange and red highlights. Someone nearby was burning their first fire of the fall in a woodstove. It was the kind of moment I dreaded ending.

"Remember I told you to bring something nice to wear?" Charlie asked.

"Of course. What do you have going on in that brilliant little head of yours?"

"I'm taking you on a date."

I smiled brightly at her. "Oh? Is that right?"

"Yes. And you'd better go get ready, because we have reservations."

I got up, walked over to her chair, and sat down in her lap like a doting teenager. "Just when I don't think I could love you any more, you surprise me."

❖

Upstairs in Charlie's small one-bedroom apartment, I took all the time I needed to—putting on makeup, drying my hair, laying out my favorite black dress I hadn't worn in years. The only thing that made me rush was the anticipation of seeing her face again.

I looked into the mirror for a long time. More than just the makeup and dress and hair, I looked happy. So happy, I almost didn't recognize the person gazing back at me.

Charlie was sitting on the couch watching a baseball game as I descended the stairs, but it was only a second before she spotted me and eagerly jumped to her feet. "You look...wow."

"What's that you kids say?" I joked, making my way slowly toward her. "You'd hit that?"

She smiled my favorite cocky smile and pulled me into her. "I'd hit that, buy a house with that, and marry that."

I laughed and kissed her hard. "You don't look so bad yourself."

She extended her arm to me. "Shall we, Dr. Jenner?"

"Absolutely."

I still had no idea where we were going as Charlie steered her car through downtown Providence.

"You aren't taking me to a diner again, are you?" I loved to tease her.

"What? You have a gripe with our first date?"

"I do recall telling you very clearly that was not a date."

"And I do recall not believing you," she shot back with a boastful grin.

I was surprised when we passed through the center of the city and continued driving.

"No, but seriously," I asked apprehensively, "where are you taking me?"

"Not out to the woods to kill you, if that's what you're thinking."

We laughed, as she suddenly pulled the car off the main road and onto a dirt strip.

"Okay, we're here." Charlie shut off the engine, and we were suddenly surrounded by darkness. "Trust me," she said, sensing my apprehension, and opened my door for me. She took my hand and led me down a short footpath. Crickets still chirped one of their last songs of the season around us, and the air was cool and clear.

"Almost there," she said.

We turned a corner, out of the dense brush that swallowed the path, into a clearing. My heart jumped and an involuntary gasp escaped me. In front of us spread a perfect view of the Providence city lights, just far enough away not to obscure the picturesque stars over our heads. I was so focused on the view in front of me, I almost missed the blanket that lay between two tree stumps covered with lit candles.

"Charlie, how did you…" I stammered, taking hold of her arm.

"Our reservations. You like them?"

I slipped my hands under her jacket and kissed her for what must have been entire days.

After the picnic dinner Charlie had had one of her medical-school friends help her make, we lay quietly on the blanket, my head on her chest, her arms as securely around me as she could get them.

We didn't speak. And as I stared up at the sky, I thought about how I'd never imagined myself as the kind of woman to fall for things like picnics under the stars. That kind of fairy-tale romance had always struck me as unnecessary and unlikely. Love, to me, had always been a practical move. Maybe I'd learned that from my parents.

But as I lay on Charlie's chest, listening to her rhythmic, even breathing and her strong, steady heart, I decided maybe I'd underestimated fairy tales and romance. Maybe it was just about finding the right story.

Chapter Twenty

I want to come to Northwood this weekend," Charlie blurted out on the phone late one night in November.

"You know you can't do that."

"Sure I can. I get in my car, hop on 146, and drive north for about thirty minutes."

I could picture her well, sitting at her dimly lit desk, smirking to herself in her sweatpants, her wild hair still damp from the shower.

"Funny. I wasn't aware they were teaching sarcasm in medical school these days."

"Hey, a lot's changed since your day, old-timer."

I laughed at her. "Careful with that 'old' business, or I'll start withholding sex."

"You wouldn't."

"Oh, but I would."

"But really, I want to visit. Michelle and some of the others have been asking me to. And I have my first free weekend coming up—"

"So you've been talking to Michelle?"

"Stop diverting, Natalie."

She was quick. And getting quicker every day she was in school. "Okay. Fine. But I have Sammy this weekend. And I'm working Saturday morning."

"Great. I haven't seen Sammy in months. And I can go visit the hospital. And…"

Charlie was growing more excited by the second, and I was losing the steam to crush her with the reality of the situation. The fact was, no one in Northwood knew about us yet. It wasn't so much that Charlie was insisting on making an announcement in the local paper or anything. But I knew she wouldn't be keen on keeping things a secret while she was there. The final custody hearing was coming up in a few weeks, and as reasonable as Peter was being about sharing our daughter, I couldn't help but feel like the slightest gust might push him over the edge.

"Charlie. If Peter finds out you're there—"

"He won't do anything, Nat. Sammy's safe with you. Besides, it's the twenty-first century. Yeah, things aren't perfect yet. But no judge is going to take custody away from you just because your damn partner was visiting you for the weekend."

"Maybe not. But it sure isn't going to look good. Not only am I freshly divorced and trying to keep my daughter, but I'm also dating a woman who's not even thirty years old?"

She replied lightly. "Well, when you put it that way…"

"It's not funny. This could ruin things."

"Don't bullshit me. I know I'm young, but I wasn't born yesterday, for Christ sake. You aren't afraid of losing Sammy. You know damn well that'll never happen. You're afraid of what the world—of what Northwood—will think when they find out Dr. Natalie Jenner is a big old lesbian."

I was silent for a long time, lying on my perfectly made-up queen-sized bed, bathing in every word she said. "I'm not that old."

There was quiet again, and then a spilling of laughter from both ends of the line.

"You know, when I'm thirty-five you'll be—"

"Don't say it, CarolAnne Thompson. Don't you dare!" We laughed some more.

"I'm serious though, Nat. You know Sammy isn't going anywhere. You're just scared of being out."

"That's not true. You and I go out in Providence all the

time. I hold your hand, and we dance, and I have absolutely no problem letting people know I'm with you."

"Yeah, but you're Providence Gay."

"You just made that up."

"Yes. But still. You're fine being out here, where nobody knows you. But in Northwood, you don't want anyone to know. You're still so deep in the closet you'd get lost trying to find your way out."

Charlie was right. I was Providence Gay. And who knew how long it would take before I was ready to be Northwood Gay too. "I'm not denying any of that."

"Look, I'm not asking you to wear rainbows, shave your head, and listen to Ani DiFranco here. Just try. A little bit—for me. Us."

"Of course I will."

"Then I'll be there Friday night."

"Can't wait." I smiled to myself.

"I love you."

"I love you too. Good night."

❖

She knocked at my door at exactly six thirty that Friday night. Sammy was busy reading her new favorite book on the floor while I ran frantically around the kitchen trying to put something decent together for dinner.

"My friend's here, sweetie. I'm going to go let her in."

"I'll help." Sammy hopped up from her place on the floor and excitedly followed me to the front door.

"Charlie!" Sammy squealed.

"Hi, Sammy!"

"That's amazing. She hasn't seen you in ages and she remembered you right away."

"What can I say? Kids love me." She flashed me a sweet, inviting smile.

"Come on, Charlie," Sammy said, grabbing Charlie's hand. "I'll show you my room."

Without missing a beat, Charlie followed Sammy upstairs. It was several minutes before they came back down.

"So, what do you think of the place?" I asked her.

"It's great. Not as swanky as the Beech Street mansion, I'm sure, but it's perfect for you two." She smiled again, and I realized that this woman I loved so dearly had hardly set foot in the home I'd spent the last decade of my life in. The home I'd raised my daughter in, studied for my boards in, laughed in, cried in, fought in, loved in. And I was momentarily further reminded of the divide that lay between what my life had been and what it was and would be from now on.

"Dinner's ready, guys." And as the three of us moved to the table, I felt as if I had a true family for the first time in ages.

"Sammy, how's my friend SpongeBob?"

"Can I go get him, Mommy? Please?" Sammy jumped eagerly from her chair.

"Sure, but don't take too long."

A few minutes later, she returned, carrying the small stuffed toy Charlie had given her in the hospital so many months earlier.

"Well, look at him. It seems like you've taken pretty good care of him."

"Yeah! He's my favorite." Sammy squeezed him tight, like she had that night in the ER.

I smiled, remembering the night we spent at Northwood when Sammy was sick. It was odd, I realized, to remember something like a GI bleed with fondness. But Sammy hadn't been sick since. It seemed her health was turning a corner. And I knew now, with some hindsight, that was the night I truly fell in love with Charlie.

I sat for a while, watching my daughter laugh at Charlie as she attempted to spin her pasta around her fork unsuccessfully.

And I couldn't help but notice how normal the whole evening was.

What was I expecting, really—that the world would cease to exist, as Pat Robertson once said, because our makeshift family suddenly did? I was ashamed of my own naïveté and ignorance. Sammy would be no worse off because of my sexuality. I hadn't become a murderer, or an alcoholic, or a drug lord. In fact, if anything, my daughter would grow up better for it. No child should live in a house with two parents who no longer loved each other. Still, I hated the idea of Sammy being known as the girl with the lesbian mom. Or maybe I was still just thinking of myself.

After dinner, we retreated to the living room to play Chutes and Ladders, until Sammy was so tired she could no longer keep her eyes open.

"Bedtime, kiddo," I said.

"Mommy?"

"Yeah?"

"I want Charlie to tuck me in." She looked pleadingly at Charlie.

"Well, that's up to her, I think."

"Of course I will. Come here." Charlie picked her up gently and carried her upstairs.

"Night, Mommy. Love you!" she called from the top.

"I love you too, baby."

"How'd it go?" I asked, once Charlie returned.

"Sleeping like an angel."

"She's crazy about you," I said, putting my arms around her waist and pulling her down beside me on the couch. "So am I."

"Likewise, Dr. Jenner," she replied, kissing me softly on my forehead and then again on my lips.

"I'm serious though. I've never seen her take to anyone like that."

"I've always had a way with kids."

"I have to tell you, I had my doubts about bringing you around Sammy. Not because I didn't know you'd be great with her. It's just confusing for her, I'm sure."

"Kids are really adaptive. You know that. All she really knows now is when Mom and Dad are happy. And really, isn't that all that should matter? She's going to grow up not knowing the difference between gay and straight, or at least not caring. That's a gift. I wish every kid could have that."

Sammy suddenly appeared at the bottom of the stairs, causing me to jump several feet away from Charlie.

"Sammy, why aren't you sleeping?" I asked, still shaking.

"I just thought of something."

"What's that, sweetie?"

"Where's Charlie going to sleep?"

Charlie and I exchanged worried glances in the midst of an awkward silence, both of us waiting for the other to respond.

"Charlie's going to sleep here, on the couch, baby. Why do you ask?" I watched Charlie's face as she raised a disappointed brow in my direction.

"She can sleep with me if she wants. I have bunk beds."

"That's nice of you, Sammy, but Charlie's going to stay here. Now go to bed. I love you."

She scurried back up the stairs, and we were once again alone. "Why'd you lie to her?"

"Oh, God, I don't know," I said with a sigh.

"Listen, she's your daughter. I wouldn't dream of telling you how to raise her. But I will say this much—the longer you keep this from her, the harder it'll be, for all of us. I mean, do you really want her to be fifteen and come home from school one day to find you half naked on this couch with your thirty-five-year-old 'friend' Charlie?"

"You're right." I grunted. "I have to tell her."

"I think you should." She put an arm around my shoulder and pulled me close to her. "I'm not really sleeping on the couch... am I?"

We laughed hard. It was the first taste of happiness I could remember, outside of my work. Upstairs, my daughter slept safely, peacefully. Next to me, on my sofa, in my home, sat the love I never thought I'd find—the love I never thought I wanted. And I found it impossible to believe I'd ever lived a day until now.

CHAPTER TWENTY-ONE

It felt good waking up next to Charlie in my big, overstuffed bed, with the late-fall sunrise peeking through the blinds. Like she'd always been there. My alarm clock went off only moments later, and her eyes opened with a smile.

"Good morning," she said, and rolled over to kiss my neck, my ears, and my chest.

"You better cut that out. I have to get to work, and God help you if I have to go in all turned on."

"Oh? And what are you doing to do about it?"

"The question is," I asked, flipping her over onto her back and pinning her, "what are you going to do about it?"

She pulled me down and kissed me hard on the mouth, running her hands up my bare back until I was dizzy with an indescribable need.

"Charlie," I breathed heavily, "I have to go."

"Tease," she said with a smirk that left my insides bursting into flames. "I'm not finished with you yet. Not by a long shot."

"That better be a promise." I kissed her once more and got up to check my phone.

"What's wrong?" Charlie must have noticed my face falling.

"The sitter banged out for today. She's sick. And Peter's in Boston visiting his sister for the weekend. I'll have to call out."

"What are you talking about? You have a sitter right here."

"You? I don't know," I said. "She can be a lot to handle."

"You said it yourself—she's crazy about me. And I adore her. Plus, I'm a medic. And a med student. You know she's safe with me. Please? Let me watch her."

I thought about it for several seconds. "You really don't mind?"

"Absolutely not. I was just going to hang around all day and watch daytime TV anyway. I'll take her to lunch, and then we'll go to the park. It's supposed to be warm today."

"Okay." I walked over and kissed her cheek. "I love you. You're amazing. Thank you so much." I undressed and headed quickly for the shower.

❖

"What's gotten into you?" Judy smiled suggestively at me from behind the nurses' desk.

"What are you talking about?"

"You're Dr. Chipper today. You handing out smiles with that Percocet too? Or maybe you're the one who's been taking the Percocet." She laughed.

"Judy, the last thing I need are rumors that I'm taking drugs. I'm just happy. Is that a crime?"

"Not at all," she said, her smile growing. "So what's he like?" Judy leaned down and whispered impatiently to me.

"What's who like?"

"The guy you're seeing. Is he tall? I bet he's tall. And hot."

"There's no guy. I swear to you."

"I won't tell. Really. You can trust me."

"I swear to you. There is no guy."

Without another word, she walked away looking nothing short of disappointed.

"You'd think she'd be a little old for that type of gossip," Michelle said suddenly from behind me.

"You heard that, huh?"

"She's back, isn't she?" For a ditzy-looking bombshell, Michelle was certainly beyond perceptive.

"I don't know what you mean."

"Charlie. She's in town."

"She told you."

"No. But it's all over your face."

Instinctively, I wiped my mouth. "Don't you have somewhere to be, Michelle? You know, sick people to tend to?" In spite of her bluntness, or maybe because of it, I'd realized over time that I really did like her.

"You're getting some!" she whispered, animatedly. "It's her. I know it. You guys are a thing now!"

"What makes you think something like that?" I said, trembling.

"You have the look." Michelle smiled at me patronizingly.

"What look is that?"

"The I'm-in-love-with-Charlie-Thompson look."

"There's a look for that?"

"Oh, yes. A very specific look. And you're screaming it."

I glanced nervously around the department, hoping desperately that no one else had caught on. In all my life, I'd never considered myself that transparent. Then again, I guess, in all my life, I'd never felt like this.

"Shit," I finally said, quietly. "Does anyone else know?"

"I think the Dr. Jenner/Charlie gossip has pretty much fizzled out since she left for Providence."

I exhaled loudly. "Thank God for small favors…"

"So, you're saying it's true? She's here?"

"Yes," I said hesitantly, "she's here."

"At your place?"

"Yes."

"And you two are…?"

"Yes! Yes. Now please, keep this to yourself, will you?"

"I may be a lot of things, Natalie," she said, sitting in the swivel chair next to me, "but I'm not a rat. And in spite of our pseudo love triangle, I want the best for her. And that's you. Let's face it. I never stood a chance. She's been in love with you from the second she stepped foot in this place."

"Really?" I smiled, gripped by the pleasure of giddy youth.

"Yes, really. I'm just glad you finally smartened up. And just so you know? No one would think any less of you for coming out. Christ, this place is full of freaks and fuck-ups. Todd Kelly had a six-month affair with Megan from X-ray until his wife found out and kicked him out of the house. Judy smokes in the staff bathroom and thinks no one can smell it. And me, well, I've always been kind of a slut." We chuckled to ourselves. "But yes, your secret is safe for as long as you want it to be."

❖

"Mommy!" I recognized Sammy's squeal from across the ED.

"Well, look who's here," I heard one of the girls from the front desk say. Even if I hadn't heard them, it would have been difficult to miss the crowd gathering around Charlie and Sammy. Abruptly, Sammy broke free of the masses and ran toward my desk.

"Whoa, Sam," Charlie called after her, "don't go running off just yet. Mom's working. Stay with me." But Sammy was already by my side.

"Hi, baby." I said, pulling her in and hugging her. "What are you doing here?"

"Charlie took me to visit you."

I glanced back to Charlie, who was being embraced by an obviously still enamored Michelle, who held on just long enough to make me frown briefly. I took Sammy's hand and led her to the group.

"So you're a babysitter now, huh, Thompson?" Jay Sabraski

was teasing her. "What's the matter? They kick you out of Brown?"

"No, Sabraski. I was just in town visiting your mom, actually."

The group roared.

"Your-mom jokes? Classy, Thompson. Classy." They laughed and hugged each other affectionately.

"But really," Judy cut in, "what are you doing with Natalie's kid?" An awkward silence flooded in around us.

"Babysitting. Obviously," Charlie said, casually. "Nata... Dr. Jenner heard I was coming to town, and her sitter's sick so she asked if I'd help."

"Begged, really," I interjected.

"Well," Judy said, "aren't you just the perfect woman."

Everyone laughed, and Michelle swooned childishly. I squeezed Sammy's shoulder, grateful for Charlie's easy charisma that seemed to distract everyone from whatever else was going on.

"How's Brown, Dr. Thompson?" one of the other nurses asked.

"Challenging. But really great."

"I expect you back here in about seven years, as our new Attending," Tim said, joining the crowd.

"I don't think you have another seven years left in you, Tim," I teased him.

"True. But you do, Natalie. You can break her in." Everyone laughed, and my faced flushed hotter than the depths of hell.

"I don't think she'll need much breaking in," I responded, trying to keep my composure. "I have to get back to work, sweetie." I bent down and kissed Sammy good-bye. "Call me if you need anything, Charlie?"

"You got it, Dr. Jenner," and I was certain I saw Michelle winking at me from several feet away.

While everyone's attention was still focused on Charlie, I

snuck out the back door, found her beat-up Nissan, and waited impatiently.

"What are you doing?" I asked as she came within earshot.

"What's the problem, Nat?"

"Sammy, get in the car, okay, sweetie?" She did so, quietly.

"You can't show up here with my daughter."

"Why not? I just wanted to visit everybody. What's so wrong with that?" It was clear she really didn't know why I was upset.

"Don't you think people will find it odd that you're babysitting Sammy?" My tone softened.

"No, actually. I don't think people will find any of this odd. In fact, I think you're the only one who does." She frowned.

A childlike shame washed over her face, and my frustration melted. "Give me a break here, Charlie." I touched her cheek. "This is new. And kind of scary."

She sighed loudly. "I know. I'm sorry. It's been a while since I've been in the closet. I guess I forgot what it's like. I need to be more patient with you."

"I said I'd try. And I'm going to. I promise. I'll do better, okay?"

"That's all I ask."

I kissed her on the cheek again, running my hand through her hair. "How's this?" I whispered in her ear.

"It's a great start." She smiled tenderly and got in the car.

❖

"Who wants pizza?" I called, nudging open the front door with my elbow.

"Me!" Sammy shrieked, sprinting to the kitchen.

"What'd you do with Charlie?" I asked, suspicious.

"We're having a birthday party for Mr. Bear."

"Oh? You are, are you?" I tried to suppress a delighted grin.

"Mmm-hmm. Come on. It's almost time for cake." I put the

box of pizza down on the counter and followed Sammy into the living room. "Sit down, Mommy."

Charlie sat cross-legged on the floor, a tiara on her head and a tutu around her waist.

"Oh, now that's just plain wrong," I said, laughing boisterously.

"Doesn't she look pretty, Mommy?"

"Oh yes, sweetie. She looks…pretty, all right." I laughed some more, as Charlie smiled at me.

"Welcome home," she said.

"Thank you." I smiled again. "Go get washed up for dinner, Sammy." They both got up and Sammy took off for the bathroom. "And as for you," I said, kissing Charlie slowly and simultaneously pulling the crown from her head, "I think it's absolutely heartwarming that you'd play dress-up with my daughter."

"Well, you know me."

"But," I said, yanking the tutu down to her ankles, "if you value your sex life, you'd be wise never to let me see you in this crap again." I laughed and kissed her one more time. Charlie had been right. Family wasn't about the perfect mother and father. It wasn't about a miserable marriage to save face. It was about love. And I had more love in that house that I'd ever before.

CHAPTER TWENTY-TWO

It was unseasonably warm for Rhode Island, as Charlie, Sammy, and I sat out on the deck by the water. The weekend was coming to a close, and I was already lonely thinking about both of them leaving that night.

"When are you coming back, Charlie?" Sammy asked, timidly.

"I don't know. Why?"

"Because I want you to."

Charlie and I smiled discreetly at each other. "I want to too. As long as it's okay with your mom, I can come back soon, okay?"

"Is it okay with you, Mom? Please? Can Charlie come back again?"

I laughed out loud. "Oh, I think we can make that happen. Now go get your things, okay, sweetie? Daddy will be here in a couple of hours."

Sammy nodded, still wound up, and ran into the house.

"I can't believe it's Sunday already." Charlie groaned despairingly.

"These weekends go by way too fast."

"You're telling me. Back to Providence...back to anatomy labs and obnoxious med students...back to life without you."

"It sucks." I reached over from my chair and took her hand.

"Sure does."

"I can't help but think how nice it'd be if we didn't have to worry about leaving."

"You mean, like living together?"

"Yeah. Like living together."

"It would be nice."

"More than nice."

We sat and silently divulged in the delicious fantasy of waking up next to each other in the morning and saying good night face-to-face, instead of over the phone thirty minutes apart. The thought was impractical, to say the least, but it was also wonderful, and inspiring, and filled a void in me I hadn't realized was still there.

"What about Wellington?"

"What about it?"

"It's perfect. Halfway between Providence and Northwood. It's a fifteen-minute drive either way. I'd be close to school. You'd be close to work, and close to Sammy. We could get a three-bedroom, and we could have an office again. I could study. We could take Sammy still. It'd be perfect." The more she talked, the more excited she became, and the harder it was going to be to tell her no.

"It would be perfect," I said.

"So let's do it!"

"Charlie. This isn't something we can just do impulsively. There's a lot to think about here. You know there's—" Peter's Chevy pulled into my driveway.

"What's she doing here?" he barked through the open window, then stepped out of his car and slammed the door.

"Shit," Charlie muttered under her breath, and stood up as if to brace herself for a fight.

"Peter, don't do anything stupid. Sammy's here." I was as calm as I could manage.

"I don't want that queer around my kid."

"Easy, Peter. There's no need for name-calling."

"You stay out of this, you got it? You're nothing but a goddamned home-wrecking dyke," he shot back.

"What the hell is wrong with you?!" I jumped up and took a quick step between them as his stance widened.

"She's what's wrong with me. It's bad enough that the fag stole my wife. Now she's out to take my kid too?"

"First of all," I said, trying to defuse the situation by blocking them from the other's view, "only guys are fags. And that's not a word I appreciate. Second of all, Peter, you sound like an uneducated redneck. I get it, you're pissed. But this is my house. And Charlie is my guest. Don't take this out on her."

"This is all your fault. My whole life has fallen to shit because you can't keep it in your fucking pants!" he shouted, looking right through me and at Charlie.

"Just calm down." Her voice shook.

"Don't talk to me like that, you bitch. I'm twice your age. And I should beat your face in right now." Before I knew what had happened, Peter had charged past me, taking Charlie by the neck and pinning her against the wall of the house.

"Peter! Get off her!" I whaled hard on his back with balled fists. "Stop it!"

"I should break your nose right now," he said, an eerie calm in his voice.

"Go...ahead and...break it then," she answered, trembling under his grip, fighting for air. "But," she whispered harshly, "it won't...change a thing..."

"Peter, please! Let her go!" I pleaded as I tried to break his hold on her.

He stared at her, hatred and a trace of fear in his eyes, and held her throat as her eyes began to widen and gloss over.

"You're killing her!"

"Fuck," he said, hostilely, and finally released his grip as Charlie fell limp to the ground. "I can't hurt you."

"A little…late…" Charlie gasped, as I dropped to her side, pushing Peter out of the way. It had never occurred to me that he'd lay a hand on me if I tried to defy him. Then again, I never thought he'd be capable of strangling Charlie either.

"Look at me! Charlie, look at me." I grabbed her drooping chin in my hand and pushed it up toward me, the physician in me taking over.

"I'm okay. Really." She was still struggling to breathe. I examined her quickly, looking in her eyes and in her mouth.

"Petechiae in your eyes and some swelling in your airway… Goddamn it, Peter! You could have killed her! She's hurt! Badly! I have to take her to the ER, and what the hell do you think I'm going to tell them?" I stood as tall as my short frame would allow me, getting so close to Peter's face our noses would have touched.

"I don't know what came over me, Natalie. I was just so angry, I—"

"What if that had been our daughter? What if Sammy had made you so angry? Would you have choked the shit out of her too?"

"Of course not!"

"Oh? And how do I know that?"

"Because!" he said, frantically, "it's Sammy!"

"We're pressing charges. And don't think this won't affect Sammy's custody. I'm going to take her from you if it's the last thing I do."

"Natalie…it's okay…" Charlie said quietly, still sitting against the wall, her breath evening.

"It's not okay." I turned back to Peter, whose eyes were filling with tears. "I cannot trust you around our child any longer. I've never seen this violent side of you before. And I'll be damned if I ever let Sammy. Now, if I were you, I'd get the hell off my property, because I'm about to pick up the phone and call the police and report you. And you can bet your weasely little ass I'll tell them right where they can find you. Go."

"But—"

"Get out!" I screamed as loudly as I could, as Peter turned and retreated like a juvenile delinquent.

"We have to get you to the hospital," I said, trying hard to hide the worry in my voice.

"Sammy?" she asked.

"Don't worry about her. We'll just tell her you're sick. She's too young to understand."

"What if she saw…" she said, concern leaking out of her words as I helped her to her feet.

"She didn't. She's in her room. I'm sure. Now wait here for just a minute, okay? I'm going to get her and we're leaving."

She nodded, too distraught to argue.

"Sammy?" I called, running into the house. "Come down here, please?" I tried my best to keep my voice simple and my expression empty as she came down the stairs, pink Disney backpack around her shoulder.

"Is Daddy here?" she asked, and tears bombarded my sight.

"No, baby. Daddy's not coming tonight, okay? You're going to stay with Charlie and me."

She paused for a minute, seemingly debating her feelings on the issue. "Okay, Mommy."

"But right now, sweetie, we have to take Charlie to Mommy's hospital."

"Is Charlie sick?"

"Well, sort of, yes. Can you be a big girl, for me and for Charlie, and come with us?"

She nodded, resolutely, and took my hand.

"Let's get you to the ER," I said quietly, holding Charlie by the waist and guiding her down the porch steps.

"I'm…fine…really," she lied.

"You are not. You know as well as I do what damage strangulation can do," I whispered sternly.

"You're the doctor," she said, forcing a smile.

We were taken back to a room immediately, but even that

couldn't stop the stares and whispers. It was no surprise, really. Charlie looked like hell. Her eyes were red with shattered blood vessels, her neck blue where Peter had held her, and she was bleeding from a small laceration on the back of her head. Still, all I found myself caring about was making sure she was all right.

As I helped her undress and slip on the gray hospital gown, my mind instantly flashed back to the night before her appendectomy, and the need to comfort, protect, and heal her took over once again. Only this time, I didn't hesitate.

"What happened?" Beth, one of the second-shift nurses, asked timidly.

Charlie looked first to me, then to Beth, and then back to me again.

I nodded quietly and took her hand. "Peter got angry... and..."

"Peter, your husband, Peter?" Beth jumped and turned to me.

"Ex-husband. But yes. Peter Anderson, for the records. I want this reported. Please make sure Tim or whoever's on calls the PD."

"Of course," she responded, appearing dumbfounded. "Charlie, I need you to tell me exactly what took place." Beth looked at us as if she was about to be caught in the middle of something she really didn't want to be part of.

"Peter showed up at Natalie's house," she said, seemingly unsure of just how much to disclose, "and he was mad...at me..."

"Why?" Beth erupted with burning curiosity.

"That...uh...doesn't matter."

"Okay. Then what happened?"

"He grabbed me by the throat, pinned me against a wall, and choked me. Really, I'm fine. Natalie's just going all 'worried doctor' on me. I'm okay. Honest."

"You shut it," I said, laughing and stroking her hair as Beth eyed us, clearly bewildered. I didn't care who was looking. I didn't care who would find out about us. That night, the reality of who my daughter's father really was had rocked me. The idea of losing Charlie had shaken me and thrown things dramatically into perspective, so outing myself to the Northwood ER didn't seem like such a big deal anymore.

"I'll send Dr. Martin in, okay?" Beth said, finally, and left the room.

"Oh, good. Martin's on. This should be fun." Charlie grunted.

"Fuck Martin."

"Dr. Jenner! What if somebody heard that filthy mouth of yours?"

I smiled and leaned in to kiss her. The sound of the plastic curtain sliding open as Jack Martin entered the room interrupted us.

"Charlie," he said, matter-of-factly, "you look terrible."

"Thanks, Dr. Martin."

"You know what I mean. Let me take a look."

As Jack probed her mouth and nose with a tongue depressor, I looked on nervously.

"She has some edema in the oral pharynx I saw earlier," I said.

"Relax, Natalie. We'll take care of her, okay? We'll get a CT and make sure she's fine." He walked out of the room.

"You think he knows what's going on?" Charlie asked.

"Jack's not stupid. Abrasive and moody maybe, but not stupid."

"People are going to find out. Your ex-husband beat the shit out of me, at your house. It's not hard to put those pieces together."

"I don't care anymore."

She looked at me apprehensively. "You don't?"

"No. I mean, I admit this isn't the ideal coming-out story. And I'm not going to get on the intercom out there and make an announcement or anything. But I'm tired of lying about the best thing in my life."

"Even if it means people thinking differently of you?"

I considered the possibility for several seconds. "If those people out there can't think beyond who's in my bed and who I love, then they aren't the people I think they are. And they can go to hell."

Charlie smiled weakly at me as I squeezed her hand. "It hurts to talk…" she said with a pitiful laugh.

"Just rest. And listen, I'm so sorry…about Peter, I mean. This is all my fault."

"Bullshit. Don't you dare blame yourself."

"I just feel awful."

"Don't. Please. I'm embarrassed enough." She looked at the floor.

"Embarrassed?"

"Yes! I talk like this big tough guy, and I get my ass handed to me by your ex-husband."

"Because you refused to fight back?"

"Well, yes. I don't make it a habit to hit people unless absolutely necessary."

"See, now that's big and tough, to me," I whispered, moving to sit down next to her on the stretcher. She lowered her head against my chest as I wrapped my arms around her and cradled her.

I saw feet under the curtain before anyone came in. And for a weak moment, I contemplated moving quickly back to the chair. But I was too tired to run anymore.

Beth entered the room and stopped so hard her shoes scuffed the floor. "Oh…I'm…Uh…Sorry…I…" She stammered repeatedly, seemingly hoping one of us would interrupt her at any moment with some kind of reasonable explanation. "It's time for your CT," she said again, coolly.

While Charlie was down the hall in radiology, I wandered out into the nurses' area, hoping to find a comforting face—someone to confide in, maybe.

"Natalie?" Jen came swinging around the corner with a bag of IV fluid in hand. "You aren't on today, are you?"

"No. I'm here with Charlie." And I waited for the bomb to drop.

"Come in here," she ordered me, pulling me into an empty exam room and making me feel like a scolded schoolchild.

"What?"

"What do you mean, you're here with Charlie?"

"You haven't heard yet? We've been here for over an hour already. I figured it'd be all over the department."

"I've been busy tonight. What happened?"

I could feel the apprehension creeping into my face as she stood waiting. "We were at my place, with Sammy—"

"What is she doing at your place? And with Sammy?"

"Jen. Just listen. We were at my place, and Peter showed up early to get Sammy. He wasn't supposed to know she was there."

"What do you mean?"

"That night you found us in the bathroom? That wasn't the first of it. And it certainly wasn't the last either." Jen rolled her eyes in distaste. "When I left Peter, I told him everything."

"Oh, sweet Mother of God," she muttered under her breath.

"Peter reacted pretty poorly and..."

"Oh, God...he..."

"Yes. I think she's okay. But she was down for a while. I'm so worried."

She was quiet for a long time, hardly seeming to breathe. "Are you going to press charges?"

"Yes, of course. I can't have him around Sammy anymore. What if that had been her?"

Jen put her arms around me and pulled me in. "I'm so sorry," she whispered into my ear.

"Thank you. I should go check on Charlie. She should be back by now." I turned and started to walk away.

"You really love her," she said, trying not to make it known how uncomfortable it made her to have to put such a sentence together. "Don't you."

"So much."

CHAPTER TWENTY-THREE

Charlie, Sammy, and I left the hospital sometime after eight that night, with Charlie, physically speaking, more or less unscathed. The swelling in her throat had ebbed, and it seemed that she would be left with little more than a badly bruised neck and ego. Try as I might to convince her Peter hadn't "won" anything, she was quiet and somnolent for the remainder of the evening. Failure wasn't an option for people like Charlie—or myself, really. And although I saw her pacifism as noble and endearing, she saw it, in this case, as defeat.

"I should have knocked his teeth in," she mumbled from the passenger seat of my Jeep on the way home.

"Then why didn't you, Charlie?"

"You really want to know?" She turned to face me, a look of anguish painting her face.

"Yes."

"Because he's Sammy's father. And that's something."

Everything in me warmed from the inside out, and I reached over and squeezed her hand. "I love you."

"I love Charlie too," Sammy shouted from the backseat. Startled that she could hear the entire exchange, I glanced at her in the rearview mirror. "You do, sweetie?"

"Yeah. She's my favorite of all your friends."

I saw Charlie smiling out of the corner of my eye. "You know, Sammy, Charlie's more than just a friend."

"Natalie, you don't have to do this," Charlie said.

"It's okay. Sammy, I love Charlie."

"You mean, like I love Grammy?"

"Sort of, baby. But more like…how mommies and daddies love each other."

I wasn't quite sure how much to tell a young child. But if I wanted my daughter to grow up thinking being gay was every bit as okay as being African, or Asian, or Jewish—thinking that we were all just human—I had to lay some kind of foundation.

"Oh," she said simply, after a long pause. "Well, that's okay too."

Charlie and I quietly chuckled, and I squeezed her hand a little tighter.

❖

We picked up Chinese on the way home, but a few bites in, Sammy was asleep with her head on my lap.

"Bedtime for all little girls," I said, picking her up and carrying her up to her room.

"Good night, Mommy. I love you. And Charlie too." And she was asleep again almost instantly.

"How are you feeling?" I asked Charlie as I made my way back down the stairs.

"Honestly? Awful. My back is killing me. I think I hit it when he tossed me against the wall."

"Let me get some ice and your Percocet."

"Wait. This is really pathetic, but I don't think I can get my arms up high enough to undress myself. Will you help?"

I smiled and started to slide her shirt over her head. "This better not just be some ploy to get me into bed."

"You'll just have to find out, I guess." She kissed me delicately.

"Come on, let's get you to bed."

I helped her up the stairs to my bedroom and guided her

to the bed and under the covers. Getting dressed again was too much effort for her sore muscles.

Containing the urge to touch her nearly naked body was almost unbearable. I'd expected, over time, that my need for her—my desire to touch her, to be close to her, to feel her—would wane. In fact, it had done the opposite. And each day, I was fairly certain I wanted her more than the day before.

"Did anyone say anything tonight? At the hospital?" she asked, groggily.

"I talked to Michelle this morning, actually."

"Oh? What did she say?"

"She said that she knew you were here and that she knew we were together. She said she was glad I'd finally smartened up. And," I said, running a finger down her smooth stomach, "she said you'd been in love with me from the minute you walked in there."

"She's a liar." Charlie laughed lightly. "I loved you from the minute I was wheeled in there. Remember?"

"That's right. I'd almost forgotten about your leg."

"When you walked into my room that afternoon, I don't think I've ever wanted to rip anybody's clothes off quite so much. I thought you were the smartest, sexiest, most, I don't know, striking woman I'd ever laid eyes on. I was done. There wasn't going to be anyone else for me ever again." She closed her eyes and smiled.

"And I thought you were a pompous little know-it-all."

"You did not."

"For the first thirty seconds or so. But then I took a minute to look at you, and not just your chart. And almost instantly, I had thoughts and feelings and wants and needs and a million other things I'd never had before."

"You did?"

"Yeah, I did. I was so insanely attracted to you, from that day forward. I couldn't pass you in the halls or look you in the eye without getting turned on. Sometimes, I'd walk into a room and didn't even have to know you were there—you have this amazing smell. It just does something to me. It always has."

"Did you know right away that I wanted you?" she asked.

"Hardly. I didn't know I wanted you, either. At least, I wasn't able to acknowledge it until the day James Pratt came in. But you? No. I never thought in a million years that some young, gorgeous woman would set her sights on me. You could have had any girl in that place."

"Now that's not true. Just Michelle."

"Just Michelle? She's a knockout. And she wanted you almost as much as I did. But you picked me."

She put her arm around me and I buried myself under her neck. "It was never a question."

The day I graduated from medical school, I thought I'd finally gotten there. But I wasn't even close.

About the Author

Emily Smith was born and raised in a small town in New Hampshire, where she started writing at an early age. Her grandmother was a children's author, and she comes from a family of English teachers. *Searching For Forever* is Emily's first full-length novel and first venture into the publishing world. When she isn't writing, which is rare, Emily works in the medical field. She has been an EMT for years and is currently in school to become a physician assistant. She lives in Boston with her partner; they try to escape to Provincetown as much as possible.

Books Available From Bold Strokes Books

Rest Home Runaways by Clifford Henderson. Baby boomer Morgan Ronzio's troubled marriage is the least of her worries when she gets the call that her addled, eighty-six-year-old, half-blind dad has escaped the rest home. (978-1-62639-169-7)

Charm City by Mason Dixon. Raq Overstreet's loyalty to her drug kingpin boss is put to the test when she begins to fall for Bathsheba Morris, the undercover cop assigned to bring him down. (978-1-62639-198-7)

Edge of Awareness by C.A. Popovich. When Marija, a woman in the middle of her third divorce, meets Dana, an out lesbian, awareness of her feelings bring up reservations about the teachings of her church. (978-1-62639-188-8)

Taken by Storm by Kim Baldwin. Lives depend on two women when a train derails high in the remote Alps, but an unforgiving mountain, avalanches, crevasses, and other perils stand between them and safety. (978-1-62639-189-5)

The Common Thread by Jaime Maddox. Dr. Nicole Coussart's life is falling apart, but fortunately, DEA Attorney Rae Rhodes is there to pick up the pieces and help Nic put them back together. (978-1-62639-190-1)

Jolt by Kris Bryant. Mystery writer Bethany Lange wasn't prepared for the twisting emotions that left her breathless the moment she laid eyes on folk singer sensation Ali Hart. (978-1-62639-191-8)

Searching For Forever by Emily Smith. Dr. Natalie Jenner's life has always been about saving others, until young paramedic Charlie Thompson comes along and shows her maybe she's the one who needs saving. (978-1-62639-186-4)

Blindsided by Karis Walsh. Blindsided by love, guide dog trainer Lenae McIntyre and media personality Cara Bradley learn to trust what they see with their hearts. (978-1-62639-078-2)

Blue Water Dreams by Dena Hankins. Lania Marchiol keeps her wary sailor's gaze trained on the horizon until Oly Rassmussen, a wickedly handsome trans man, sends her trusty compass spinning off course. (978-1-62639-192-5)

Let the Lover Be by Sheree Greer. Kiana Lewis, a functional alcoholic on the verge of destruction, finally faces the demons of her past while finding love and earning redemption in New Orleans. (978-1-62639-077-5)

About Face by VK Powell. Forensic artist Macy Sheridan and Detective Leigh Monroe work on a case that has troubled them both for years, but they're hampered by the past and their unlikely yet undeniable attraction. (978-1-62639-079-9)

Blackstone by Shea Godfrey. For Darry and Jessa, the chance at a life of freedom is stolen by the arrival of war and an ancient prophecy that just might destroy their love. (978-1-62639-080-5)

Out of This World by Maggie Morton. Iris decided to cross an ocean to get over her ex. But instead, she ends up traveling much farther, all the way to another world. Once she's there, only a mysterious, sexy, and magical woman can help her return home. (978-1-62639-083-6)

Kiss The Girl by Melissa Brayden. Sleeping with the enemy has never been so complicated. Brooklyn Campbell and Jessica Lennox face off in love and advertising in fast-paced New York City. (978-1-62639-071-3)

Taking Fire: A First Responders Novel by Radclyffe. Hunted by extremists and under siege by nature's most virulent weapons, Navy medic Max de Milles and Red Cross worker Rachel Winslow join forces to survive and discover something far more lasting. (978-1-62639-072-0)

First Tango in Paris by Shelley Thrasher. When French law student Eva Laroche meets American call girl Brigitte Green in 1970s Paris, they have no idea how their pasts and futures will intersect. (978-1-62639-073-7)